S

SCEPTRE

Also by Shyama Perera

Haven't Stopped Dancing Yet

Bitter
Sweet
Symphony

SHYAMA PERERA

SCEPTRE

Thanks to Natasha Maw for appearing on the jacket.

First published in 2001 by Hodder and Stoughton
A division of Hodder Headline
A Sceptre Book

10 9 8 7 6 5 4 3 2 1

A CIP catalogue record for this book is available
from the British Library

ISBN 0 340 76703 0

Typeset by Palimpsest Book Production Limited,
Polmont, Stirlingshire
Printed and bound in Great Britain by
Mackays of Chatham PLC, Chatham, Kent

Hodder and Stoughton
A division of Hodder Headline
338 Euston Road
London NW1 3BH

For David
Because mostly, it was brilliant

PART ONE

TODAY

Confession is an act of violence against the innocent

∫

An old joke.

The devil flags down a lawyer. 'Psst: get this. I'll give you unlimited professional success; the freedom to do whatever you want; and – as the icing on the cake – endless, *fantastic* sex. All I want in return is your soul, your wife's soul, the souls of your children, your parents, your in-laws, and your friends.'

Confused, the lawyer scratches his head. After a moment he turns: 'So what's the catch?'

This morning, my adored husband of ten years, told me he was in love with someone else. Then he went, leaving me with our two small children aged seven and three.

They think he's working late, but as I write he's sharing a bed with his mistress – a single bed in her sister's flat, soiled with the semen of history foregone.

Tomorrow he will call and ask me if a vaginal orgasm can go undetected. I will tell him that if *She'd* had a vaginal orgasm, She'd know. But that's tomorrow; and I am not yet recovered from the body blow of today.

We were getting up when he, Buster, rolled over and held me: 'What do you think's going wrong in our marriage?'

I nosed into the familiar thicket of sandy, warm chest-hair: 'I've been at home too long. It's getting me down. I'm sorry if I'm taking it out on you, Buster. I know you're worried about money. I'll find ways to reduce the bills.'

He sighed and pulled away: 'If only it were that simple.'

Something in his manner disturbed me. Suddenly, inexplicably, I was cold inside. We both lay absolutely still.

I said: 'Are you having an affair?'

'No,' he replied. 'It's worse than that.'

I closed my eyes. Our children were playing outside the bedroom door. Today is Lilla's class assembly and she is the star. We're all going. Jack's skipping nursery. Buster turned back towards me. On the landing there was sudden amnesty; momentary silence.

He said: 'I'm in love with someone else and I don't want to be here any more.'

When we married, I told Buster that if he even kissed another woman, I'd cut off his bollocks and hang them from the gate. I sensed his anxiety at that moment, as, in a series of flashes, the peculiar fragments of emotional jigsaw recently scattered round the house come together to make a horror movie whole. I remembered the two-hour trips to Homebase for one screwdriver or a packet of pipe lagging; the internet obsession; the tarot card reading. He'd even started listening to Radio One, for God's sake!

I said: 'Is it someone I know?'

'You met her once. It's Christine Brown.'

A vague picture from years back comes to mind. 'Have you slept with her?'

'No. We've just been meeting for lunch.' A pause. 'We've kissed.' Such pride.

'Was it good?'

'Yes.' A laugh.

'How long has it been going on?'

'Four months.'

Jack and Lilla were playing Hide and Seek, feet pounding down the corridor, squeaks and giggles: 'Got you!'

'Does Christine feel the same?'

'Yes.'

'And what is it you want to do?'

'I'm moving out. Christine and I will live apart for six months, then we'll get a flat nearby – so I can see the kids.'

Just like that.

I listened to these jump cuts as if they were happening to someone else. I still feel like that now. It's like a near-death experience. Except I'm fully conscious. In this state of half-being, I reasoned that he wouldn't give up ten years of happiness and six months of strain for one hundred and twenty days of occasional lunching. That it was fantasy; an escape.

I said: 'I really envy you, Buster. Falling in love is such a wonderful feeling, but you mustn't let it destroy what we have. There are two children here who need you. Whatever's going wrong with us is only a blip. We can put it right.'

He pulled away: 'You don't understand, Nina. It's what I want. I've already decided.'

When things go wrong in a marriage, nobody tells. Marriage is a social investment. We put in love, trust, loyalty, finance; and draw out children, companionship, community. The happy couple is the pound sterling and their friends, family and colleagues are the City. When the pound is buoyant, the City is happy. When the pound fluctuates, all City investments suffer a ripple effect.

In the parched milliseconds after Buster's announcement, I thought of my mother; of his parents; of dear friends who smiled upon our marital bliss. I thought of the bank manager upping my overdraft; of the carpets being paid on HP; of the neighbour whose shed roof he'd promised to fix. All of these and a thousand others who would be touched by any fall-out. I looked across to our wedding photo on the dressing table and imagined all the smiling faces crumpling in disbelief.

What was Marc Bolan's greatest hit?
    A tree.

I have faint memories of my Aunty breaking down when Jim Reeves perished in a plane crash. I remember friends laying flowers at the tree in Barnes, where Marc Bolan met his end. Every moment of the day John Lennon was murdered is fresh in my mind. They played 'Imagine' on the radio and I couldn't stop crying.
    Seminal moments in popular culture are retained for ever.
    Later, people will recount *their* experience of the death of Buster and Nina's marriage. It is the shattering of a glass in which we all see our self-image.
    I held on to my husband, smelling his earthy early morning-ness, and vainly trawled through the various options. I love you. Please don't leave me. Please don't leave *us*.
    Buster said: 'It's seven thirty. We'd better rush.'
    I got out of bed wondering how our lives could have changed for ever in the course of a dozen sentences.

Lilla wants to wear a special dress: 'I'm not going to stand up in front of everyone in a school sweatshirt.'
    'But Sweetheart, what does it matter—'
    'I won't wear it!'
    Buster shouts: 'For God's sake let her wear what she wants.' He is in Jack's room, wrestling porky little legs into corduroy trousers. Somewhere in between we've had

breakfast. I have no recollection of it. He packed a school lunch-box and hummed over a bowl of Sainsbury's Luxury Muesli: Robbie Williams, 'Let Me Entertain You'.

I stand at Lilla's window looking out on to the garden. It is January. The grass is long and unkempt. The new turf we laid down last summer in a furious flurry of 'f' words has merged with the old to create a boggy whole: London's clay soil. Along the sides there's a sparse trail of winter jasmine. The vermillion stalks of the dogwood provide the only colour in the flowerbed. At the back, the blue slide has been turned upside. The elastic that held the trampoline together is frayed and broken. An old pink Barbie bike is leaning against my newly planted weeping birch and rusting in the rain.

Lilla has pulled out her red dress and is watching me: defiant, uncertain. I shrug and go to the shower.

This time tomorrow he will have bedded her three times. He will boast to me about it, forgetting the passion which once fired *us*. He will tell me about her husband, whom she leaves after the consummation. He'll pass on her sexual preferences.

So many confidences, Buster, and I'll sit and listen because I'm still your best friend and still I can't hurt you.

Once, when it was fashionable, one of the office telephonists, a shapely middle-aged woman, did a streak around our desks.

One of the young guys shouted: 'Get yourself a new dress Martha – that one needs ironing.'

In the bathroom I inspect my saggy old body through dull eyes. I wish I'd done some exercise; refused that second after-dinner mint; restyled my thinning fringe – he mentioned that a lot.

I examine myself minutely. I am not a prime specimen. I am not even a specimen in my prime. Yet still, like the prisoner facing the firing squad, I'm searching for a reprieve.

I pull in my stomach, as if with that single act, I can have it patted flat and sorted by the time my husband returns tonight.

Every time there's a medical scare I'm convinced I've got it. Herpes, Aids, cancer, pleurisy – I can always conjure up an instance where I've displayed most of the symptoms.

'You've got a death wish, Nina,' my sister said, one day.

'No, not a death wish. It's just that I've been so bloody lucky in my life, I'm always waiting for something to go wrong.'

'Why can't you just enjoy it for what it is?'

'Because it doesn't seem fair, Maddie. I got the career I wanted, I got the man I wanted, I got the children I wanted – the home, the car – everything.'

'Not the figure.' She cut into a lemon tart and we laughed. 'Anyway, someone's got to have it all. Why not you?'

Sometimes when I'm driving up the M1, I have an inexplicable urge to take my hands off the wheel. My friends have similar experiences – standing at the edge of tube station platforms, willing themselves to topple over; leaning that little bit too far over a balcony; picking up an implement mid-argument and wondering what would happen if you used it.

Tempting fate gives one control.

It's not so easy when fate tempts you.

I said: 'Something's got to go wrong somewhere along the line – it's the law of averages.'

'But you're not average,' Maddie replied.

I follow Buster and Jack up the back stairs of St Saviour's

school and enter the assembly hall where 3L are lined up for their performance. We sit at the front, but my focus is skewed; and as Lilla jumps up and introduces her class, not knowing what her beloved father plans, I feel the first set of tears move into place.

My daughter is not a theatrical natural. Self-conscious in her red dress, she is at a stage-prop blackboard leading her friends in song: I danced in the morning when the world was begun, and I danced with the moon and the stars and the sun. Fresh faces, sweet voices; so much shining hair.

Lilla catches my eye shyly and I smile. She looks proudly across to her father bouncing Jack on his knee. I turn away. One of the other mothers gives me a wave. I reply with a vague facial gesture.

My husband is in love with another woman and is going to leave.

How can a man tell that his wife's dead?
Sex is the same, but the dishes pile up.

In recent weeks, Buster has been like a squaddie in a brothel. He has strong-armed me into some strange sexual practices. He has surfed the Net for porny pictures. He's been on a testosterone high. One night I said to him: 'If this is the result of tension in other areas of our marriage, it's a substantial pay-off.'

Then, two nights ago, I exploded: 'Buster, what is your function in this house?' He was confused. I said: 'You shout at the children, you ignore me, you spend hours in the study. If I could earn as much as you, what would your FUNCTION be?'

He turned away: 'We should never have bought this house.'

Does a man fall in love with another woman because he doesn't like his house?

In a couple of weeks I will ask him what he loves about Christine. He'll tell me that she gives him space; doesn't criticise; and is interested in everything he does.

Then I will realise that Buster's leaving has nothing to do with me. It is all about him. But that's in a couple of weeks: and I'm still sitting in the school hall with my family.

A man goes into the doctor's surgery.

She says: 'What's the trouble, Mr Roberts?'

He undoes his trousers, pulls out the most massive plonker and lays it across the table like a hose.

'Dear God!' she exclaims. 'What's the matter with it?'

'Nothing Doctor: but it's a beauty, isn't it?'

We call my mother with some excuse and drop Jack at her flat. Back home, Buster says: 'I have thirty minutes. If you want to talk, I'll listen.'

It is four hours since we woke up. Four months since he started seeing Christine. Ten years since we publicly committed ourselves to each other. We go to the kitchen. I watch as he sits down. I look at his beloved frame: the unruly blond tufts receding at the crown; the small upturned nose; the constant smile around his mouth. He's getting a paunch but it's hidden under well-cut trousers. I put on the kettle. Buster is jaunty: full of purpose. I suddenly realise that he's already lived this moment a thousand times. That he is not fearful, but relieved.

My husband is a man who has lectured the chattering classes on family values across dinner tables from Flask Walk to Tredegar Square; a man who did not just thump the tub of righteousness, but helped design it over grilled peppers at the River Café.

Later, Maddie will ask: 'How did you not guess, Nina?'

And I'll say: 'Because he was still Buster. He gave the kids a bath, moaned about work and studied holiday brochures in bed.'

I have walked down the long gallery of philandering husbands and looked closely at their faces – from President Kennedy to Tommy Cooper, from Roger Moore to Lyle Lovett. There is nothing that marks out one from the other; or that marks them out from those who don't. No Lombroso-esque facial signature, no untrustworthy gleam in the eye: no curious bulge in the fly area.

Maddie says: 'Surely his behaviour changed?'

'Of course it did, but only over the last few weeks and, as you know, he's been grumpy about work for ages. I did ask playfully if there was someone else, but he looked me in the eye and said "no".'

'And you believed him.'

'He was my husband, Sis. I loved him. He loved me.' I push away my half-eaten plate of chicken liver parfait: 'We were a unit. Why shouldn't I have believed him?'

There is a perverse logic that connects the homophobe to latent homosexuality; the celibate priest to dark carnal longing. Women often belittle men who spurn their sexual advances; children pick on those most like them. We project negative feelings on to people who remind us of our own weaknesses.

Occasionally, when Buster was eliciting a promise of lifelong monogamy from me, I'd tease him: 'Why are you so worried, Buster. Is it because you think *you* might stray?' And we'd laugh because we were so certain of our future.

I am dead inside, yet the options and processes are clear in my mind: as if I've waited for this day all my life. I say:

'Buster, please don't act hastily. Even if our marriage is over, the children and I need time to accept it. If nothing else, stay for three months; make a final effort. Not for me: for them. If you still want Christine at that stage – go with my blessing.'

He shakes his head: 'It's out of control. I *have* to be with her.'

'Buster, Lilla and Jack worship you. I can see now, why you've been so jumpy with them – but *they* won't know that. If you go, they'll blame themselves.'

'They'll get over it. Children are more resilient than you think.'

'As long as I'm here to pick up the pieces?'

'They'll see me all the time. You won't want for anything.'

I shout: 'This isn't about MONEY, Buster. Reject me if you must, but not our children. You can't sacrifice them for a *woman*!'

'I'm sorry, Nina, but I'm not willing to sacrifice myself.'

What do you do when you see your wife crawling on the lawn?

Reload.

I say: 'This isn't fair, Buster. Your whole legal career has been about giving a voice to cheats and murderers. You've fought for their rights. If you walk away without giving our marriage a chance, *you're* committing the gravest injustice of all.' He says nothing. 'What about Christine's husband?'

'He's a bastard. He doesn't deserve her.'

We sit in silence for some moments. Finally he says: 'I'm not proud of myself, but there it is.'

Cliché speak: an exclamational shorthand that expresses the extremes of emotional confrontation.

I say: 'Buster, remember Mark Landsman? When I was dating him, it was like a drug. We couldn't get enough of each other. I felt out of control – like you do now. We were both free, but in the end the intensity of it frightened us. It was so obsessive: like baboons sniffing each other's bottoms; unreal; base.'

'It's not like that with Christine.'

'If it wasn't, would you be walking out? *Think of Lilla and Jack.*' He sighs dramatically. I say: 'Look Buster, don't you think I sometimes yearn for another man's arms around me? Don't you think I look back and wonder "what if?" In ten years' time, Christine will still come into your thoughts: that doesn't mean our marriage is a mistake.'

'I don't want to argue, Nina. This was *meant.*'

Desperately, I start to beg. 'If it's true love, Buster, she'll wait. Don't stay for ever – let's just have one go at putting it right. For old times' sake if nothing else.'

Buster stares out of the window, bored. 'You can't legislate for matters of the heart. This is what I want.' He pulls himself out of the chair: 'Looks like rain – I'd better call a cab.'

But surely, Buster, marriage is proof that you *can* legislate for matters of the heart. That love can be structured and given a purpose; that by harnessing emotion in a positive way, it becomes socially cohesive.

The reason we married was that we believed in that institution. There were no shotguns in the church on our wedding day; no ex-girlfriends mouthing obscenities when the priest threw out the line about lawful impediments. We loved each other; we wanted a family; commitment. To buy into the system.

We promised, remember? For richer for poorer, in sickness and in health. And we were so happy – because we knew *we* would never become a sad divorce statistic.

Sometimes, something that is absolutely right, can feel utterly wrong. That's the way life plays its cards.

Like the sweet little polar bear who lisps: 'Mummy, am I *really* a polar bear?'

His mother kisses him: 'Yes of course you are, my darling – every furry inch of you.'

The next day, over breakfast, he looks up uncertainly: 'Mummy, am I *really* a polar bear? Are you sure I'm not a grizzly bear or a brown bear?'

'Darling child, I promise you are every inch a polar bear.'

This continues for some days. Finally, one morning, the little chap whines: 'Mummy, what if you're wrong and I'm really a koala bear or a Pooh bear? Not a polar bear at all?'

She nuzzles his soft white head: 'Darling, from your ears to your toes, you are very definitely, absolutely and utterly, a little polar bear.'

'In that case,' her son shouts miserably: 'Why am I always so BLOODY COLD?'

When Buster has gone I pick up the phone and call Maddie. No answer. I put it down and stare out of the window, numb.

I ring Mala. I say: 'Mala, Buster's in love with another woman and he's leaving us.'

She says: 'What do you mean?'

'He told me this morning. He's been seeing someone else for four months. He doesn't want to be married to me any more.'

There is a terrible silence. Finally my best friend says, chokingly, stupidly: 'But that doesn't mean he's leaving.'

I scream: 'But he IS leaving. He says it's over.' And then I start to howl like a distressed animal. I am keening uncontrollably down the phone and she lacks the necessary tools to help me: a crowbar to jemmy Buster back through the door, a hammer to nail him into place, a Banham security lock to prevent his escape.

Mala knows about husbands. She's lost two. Her three children are ferried between them on alternate weekends. Her first husband ran off with a childless peroxide doxy because he couldn't stand the noise and impositions of fatherhood. The second, a sculptor, burned out within two years of their marriage. 'He hasn't sold a thing in that time and he's always pissed. I can't be caring for the children and him, Nina.'

We've spent many nights, both happy and sad, gazing into the bottom of a glass, trying to make sense of the world. Of her fractured world and my secure one. She hasn't seen the film or got the T-shirt, but she did, ironically, write a book called *Romantic Love* which topped the bestseller list for six months.

I've complained to her about Buster in recent weeks but she was dismissive: 'Listen, Nina, all men have dark periods. Compared to the people around *me*, you and Buster are honeymooners: the editor screws every woman with an A'level; my secretary's stalking the head of marketing; and the fashion ed has secretly aborted her husband's baby so she won't miss the spring shows. Buster being bolshy is *not* the end of the world.'

If it's not the end of the world, it is at least the crashing of two tectonic plates beneath a continent. The creation of a deep and jagged fissure into which large swathes of our lives will collapse like an anthill to be swallowed up seamlessly.

Now Mala, her voice breaking, is saying: 'Don't panic. It's early days.'
'He'll never find a woman as bright or as beautiful as you, Nina.'

'That isn't the point.' I sniff and wipe away the last of this particular batch of tears. 'Anyway, Buster's too proud. He couldn't bear to lose face. If he goes, he'll never come back.'

Mala too is tearful: 'I'm so sorry, Nina. So sorry.'

The conspiracy of silence surrounding marriage is like the information vacuum women have constructed around childbirth. They teach you to get on all fours and puff puff blow. They describe the misery of labour as *productive pain*. They wheel out the odd soul who survived unscathed as testimony of the womanly – the motherly – ideal.

It's not like slipping a disc and spending a fortnight peeing into a roasting tin. No, they'll say, at the end of twelve or twenty-four hours of hideous suffering, there'll be a cute little bundle in your arms. The bleeding; the stitches; the fear when using a toilet; will all be worth it. *Refuse pain relief.*

I tell everyone that half the natural birthers I know ended up having forceps or emergency Caesarians. In life, you should take all the help you can get.

Later, I'll ask Buster, the man who's rediscovered passion, if sex with Christine is better than sex with me. Time and again he'll look down and refuse to answer. Then, one day, during a row, he turns round and shouts: 'At least it isn't like putting my prick in the Blackwall Tunnel!'

I say: 'That's because I had your children, Buster. Five years down the line, Christine will be the same.'

In fairness, he'll apologise: 'I didn't mean it. You know that. Honestly.' But the damage is done.

That's another thing the sisterhood doesn't tell you.

Things are not always as they seem.

A man goes into a pub with a frog on his head.

The barman says: 'Bloody hell! How did that happen?'

The frog replies: 'I really don't know. It *started* as an abscess on my arse.'

'What do I tell the kids, Mala?'

'That you've been arguing. That you need a break from each other.' She sighs. 'The usual thing. Oh God, Nina, I'm so sorry. I know what you're feeling. I wouldn't wish it on my worst enemy. Is he coming home tonight?'

'At eight. He said he knew I had a lot to say. He said he'd listen, but I had to understand there was no going back.' Again, I am crying.

Her voice softens: 'If it's only been four months . . . he's hitting forty . . . this is just a mid-life crisis.'

We both know she is filling the space that Buster will later claim is better provided by Christine.

No, it's not space. It's a void.

Outer space.

With hindsight, I will recognise the marked difference in male and female perceptions of what constititutes space.

For me, it was the freedom to express myself within the security of an established unit: the opportunity for us *both* to be selfish and concentrate on our individual needs.

For Buster, it was time for *him* to be selfish while I remained on hand: alert, approachable and attentive to *his* individual needs.

Mala says: 'Even if you don't want me to come over, Nina, I think I should. You may have lost your husband but you've still got your friends. Debbie can do morning conference. I'll get a cab.'

'It's all right,' I say. 'I can see Mum coming up the garden path with Jack.'

Jack is a boy. This means that he talked later than his sister because boys are slower to pick up language. It means he'll spend hours playing with the same toy: running Thomas the Tank Engine up and down the kitchen table or sitting in a corner with a drum. He has watched the same Postman Pat video dozens of times in the past week.

At his age, three, his sister played interactive games with several friends simultaneously. Jack runs around popping guns or chasing balls irrespective of whether his play-mates are part of the same activity. He is focused only on himself.

If I admonish him for spitting or hitting, he smiles sweetly and kisses me. I forgive him immediately. Lilla would have argued her corner, shouted that she hated me and stomped from the room. She still does. Boys learn early that women are secretly flattered by the Male Gaze; girls, that they're tough adversaries.

Jack, in other words, has been fashioned a man by nature, not nurture. Already he has the characteristics that one thinks of as typically male. This does not detract from his charm – it adds to it. He is an enigma to me. An exciting, aloof, sensuous bundle who lavishes affection in the gaps his sister fills with words. An essentially uncomplicated being whose lack of guile makes him appear deeply complex to the female mind.

Women cannot accept that there is so little to unravel in men.

And, indeed, such a paucity of material on which to effect change.

My mother looks at me curiously, but I am all mopped up. I say: 'Mum, can you keep Jack out a bit longer? I've some business to sort out.'

As one door closes, others open.

A doctor approaches an old man in his hospital bed. 'Mr

Jones I'm terribly sorry to tell you that I have some bad news. But I also have some good news. Which do you want first?'

The old man sighs: 'I'll take the bad news please, Doctor.'

'The bad news is, we have to amputate both your feet.'

'Oh my God! What can the good news be?'

'The man in the next bed wants to buy your slippers.'

I go to the bathroom and vomit. Sitting on the floor by the toilet, I call Buster's mother on the cordless phone and tell her. Stunned, she says: 'Momentary madness. Buster isn't that sort of man. He loves you, Nina. He adores Lilla and Jack. This is pure stress. He'd never go.'

We cry together: the good woman who fashioned Buster to be someone special, and the distraught woman who will shoulder the blame for his downfall.

Afterwards I go into the kitchen and frenetically start rearranging cupboards, rinsing dead flies out of forgotten cups and stacking the Pyrex. In the weeks that follow, order will be restored to every corner of the house, from the bathroom cabinet to the CD rack. I put one on now, to drown the sound of sobbing that seems to be coming from somewhere else: Natalie Imbruglia. I can see my perfect sky is torn.

For weeks I've been asking Buster what's wrong. Two days ago, when I asked him what his function was, I introduced the D word for the first time: 'If you don't lighten up, Buster, we may as well divorce.' And instead of laughing or saying sorry, he pounced on it. 'Okay, if that's what you want. Why *don't* we get divorced?'

The following morning – yesterday morning – he said: 'Do you want to take back anything you said last night?'

I said: 'Do you?'

'I'll hear what you take back first.'

But then Jack cried out because Lilla changed the video, and the conversation, if that's what it was, terminated.

As I arrange saucepans in order of size, I think of the times Buster has engineered confrontations over recent weeks; perhaps hoping I'd snap and provide the impetus for him to go. Would he have mentioned Christine then, or claimed she arrived later? I do not know. I do not care.

All I want is to push her through his system like a dog being wormed.

The phone goes. It's Maddie.

'Nina? I didn't understand your message. Are you all right?' I tell her. There's silence. Indefinable silence. Then she says very quietly: 'The bastard.'

Two guys and a girl sit down in a bar.

The first guy says: 'I suppose I'm a Yuppie. You know: Young, Urban Professional.'

The second laughs: 'And I'm a Dink. You know: Double Income, No Kids.'

They turn to the woman: 'And what are you.'

She shrugs: 'Oh I'm a Wife. You know: Washing, Ironing, Fucking, Etc.'

Maddie says: 'Who else knows?'

'Just Mala and Buster's mother, Kate.'

'Don't mention it to anyone else. It may blow over. You don't want half the neighbourhood knowing your business.'

'Thanks for that.'

'Oh Nina, I'm just trying to think ahead.' Maddie: a true carrier of the Sutra family bloodline; practical to the last. We pick over the scant details. She is upset beyond measure. She says: 'I'm going to call Buster at work and make him come to his senses!'

'That'll make it worse.'
'Then I'll get Gavin to call him.'
'No!'
'Why not?'
'Because you and Gavin are part of what he's escaping.'

Later Buster will tell me that the ten days of Christmas, when he couldn't contact Christine, were the worst of his life. That while the kids played with their presents and our mothers swapped stories; while Maddie and I made decorations and friends drank Blanquette de Limoux beneath our tree; while Boney M sang 'Mary's Boy Child' and Lilla and Jack strung Christmas cards around the front hall, he'd secretly been drinking gin in the kitchen. 'I only got through it by being blind drunk, but you didn't notice.'

No, Buster, I didn't notice. I was too busy making up for your indolence. What was it you said? 'I hate Christmas. I hate having all these bloody people in the house. We see too much of family and friends without this bloody razzamatazz.'

Anyway, you may think you were blitzed, but there was still some gin left when I checked out your story.

So you're capable of romanticising too.

When Maddie married Gavin, nobody thought it would last. He was easy-going and she was so controlled. Now they have children and two careers, a beautiful home and a comfortable mutual tolerance: but they haven't slept together for nearly three years. 'We're friends. That's worth so much more.'

'But Maddie, you're only thirty-four!'

She shrugs: 'It just doesn't happen. We've talked about it: it isn't a problem. We're not unusual you know.'

'Aren't you scared he'll go off with someone else?'

'What, Gavin? Don't be ridiculous, Nina.' She stops quartering oranges and thinks for a moment: 'Marriage is more than sex.'

'I believe that too, but I can't imagine not sleeping with Buster, even if the earth doesn't always move.'

'That's it precisely,' Maddie says. 'It doesn't does it? There's no spontaneity with kids.' She arranges the orange segments into a series of five-point stars. 'We're permanently exhausted.'

Sex within marriage is not all it could be. The sense of abandon lovers experience in the early years is eroded by the mundane minutiae of everyday living. In the fact that we get older and tire more easily. In the white noise of responsibility: the routines, the set-pieces, the chores. At some point predictability fells mystery in a spectacularly uneventful *coup de grâce*. But familiarity need not breed contempt. In a good marriage, it breeds contentment: an absolute sense of self-knowledge.

I consider Maddie and her tray of fruit. 'Sex does matter. It's a sort of barometer of where you're at.'

'Then clearly,' she says drily, 'Gavin and I are off the scale.'

Is a happy marriage tangible or just a state of mind? When do two people living through the same set of circumstances start perceiving them differently?

Later I'll ask Mala: 'Why do *you* think Buster went?'

'Sex. He was quite happy until he got a sniff of Christine. Men and their willies are unpredictable, Nina.'

'But all he's doing with her, is replicating life with me.'

'But not life with the children. Yet. Maybe, like Jay, he'll end up miserable with an unplanned second family, but right now it's hands-free motoring.'

Maddie butts in: 'He's jumped from the frying pan into the fire.' Sprinkling cocoa powder on to a hand-whisked chocolate mousse she purses her lips: 'A woman complained saying she couldn't get this recipe right. I can't work out where she went wrong.'

'Ignore it.'

She raises a practised eyebrow: 'I need to understand. The secret's in the detail. Beat it half-heartedly, the mixture collapses; beat it too hard and it sets like rock.' She puts the confection in the fridge. 'If Buster had calculated his checks and balances, he'd still be here.'

Suddenly I understand why people have affairs. And, in the cold light of today, it seems a much more humane way of dealing with our need for variety, fun and fucking without baggage.

At three o'clock, Mum returns Jack. 'What's wrong, Darling?'

I smile through swollen eyes: 'Shellfish allergy.'

A mother quizzes her daughter on her new boyfriend: 'I'm sick of the irresponsible louts you bring back! What sort of man is Ken? Does he have his own home? Is he respectable?'

'Of course he is Mum. He's got a fabulous house in the suburbs, a successful wife and three really-well-brought-up children.'

Jack and I drive down to pick up Lilla from school.

She's eating a piece of cake – a celebration of this morning's class performance. 'Did you see me, Mummy?'

'Of course I saw you.'

'Was I good?'

'Yes, Precious, you were brilliant.'

We walk back across the playground.

'Which bit did you like best?'

'All of it.'

'But which bit specially?'
'The beginning.' It's all I can remember.
'Why?'
The playground lady says: 'Is that your car Mrs Goodholme? You shouldn't really park it on the zig-zags.' Mrs Goodholme. For how much longer? I smile and walk by.
'Why?'
'Why what, Lilla?'
'Why did you like the beginning best?'

I like beginnings because they're so full of promise. The first page of a book, the first day of a job, the first time you buy yourself flowers, the first date with a new man, the first touch, the first kiss, the first surprise in the ghost train, the first kick of a good liqueur, the first moment you hold your own baby. I like beginnings because I know there's always more to come.

Unlike endings, when it all suddenly stops.

Soon Lilla will write me a note: 'Dear Mum I love you I love you a lot. But I can't wait till tomourow (sic) when Daddy comes. I love him a lot. I wish he was still here. Love me.'

And she will ask: 'Mummy, if there were five dwarves who wanted to marry you and they were all equally ugly, which one would you choose?'

I say: 'Well, it's not much of a choice.'

'What if one of them said he'd never shout at you and would always be nice to you?'

'Then I suppose I'd choose that one.'

She wants a father. 'Mummy, please will you marry again? If you married, he'd *have* to read me bedtime stories.'

Somehow it is six o'clock and I have cooked spaghetti bolognese. Lilla and Jack eat appreciatively, confused by my sudden absences from the kitchen. At one point, when I am again crying on the phone to Maddie, Lilla comes into the bedroom and hugs me: 'I love you, Mummy. Don't be sad.'

At seven o'clock they are in the bath.

At seven twenty, I am drying their precious bodies and putting them into pyjamas.

At seven thirty, we are choosing their bedtime books and tapes when the phone rings. 'Nina? Buster. I'm going for a drink with Ray. I'll be back about eleven.'

I think: is he really meeting Ray, or is he meeting Christine? I say: 'You can't do that, Buster. We need to talk.'

'We can talk tomorrow.'

'Tomorrow's Saturday. The children will be here.' Silence. 'Please, Buster, come home. If we mean anything to you, come home. I'm going crazy. I can't tell anyone. I can't ask for help. This is cruelty. We have to talk.'

'I've arranged it now. I'll see you later.'

In every marriage more than a week old, there are grounds for divorce. The trick is to find, and continue to find, grounds for marriage. (Robert Anderson.)

At this minute, Maddie is concocting some sort of cheese soufflé for a Sunday supplement special pull-out. 'I'll be done by eight thirty, then we can talk more.' Gavin is doing something structural with the Millennium Dome. They're up against a deadline and he's coming home later and later. Susannah, their nanny, is making enough on overtime to buy a white-water-rafting holiday in Peru. 'It's sod's law: I've given Susannah the night off.'

'That's all right. I don't want company.'

Mala, too, is threatening to come over. She has rekindled a friendship with the brother of an old friend; a morose but good-looking Chinese man. Tonight they're at a gallery opening. 'It's seven till nine. I'll call you afterwards.'

I put the children to bed. Numb. No, I'm already numb.

Number. Everything I have dreamt about, planned for and taken for granted these past ten years is collapsing around me. Happy moments from the past glide by on a conveyor belt, like longed-for prizes on *The Generation Game*: toaster, mixer, crate of champagne, cuddly toy. Frantically, I consign them to memory.

We met on a Friday. I was wearing pink suede boots and a purple dress under a pink and black sweater. Well, it was the eighties! Buster had just started as a solicitor with Carters – known to the local criminal fraternity as Farters – in Camden Town. He was drinking in a retrograde spit-and-sawdust pub called The Monarch when I turned up with a couple of fellow copywriters from BCAF – Bugle Casey Avedon Flaherty. It was lust at first sight.

Somehow we got talking and left our respective groups.

We climbed into his Alfa Romeo and went drinking at the Bass Clef.

We didn't listen to the music. We sat in the outer area and ordered food. We kept leaning across the table towards each other. Closer and closer, heads touching and suddenly pulling away. Giggly, yearning, drunk.

He wasn't really my type: large and fair. He had a silly name – after the comic actor, his father's favourite – and he was a little bit too full of himself. But there was something uplifting about him. He was a self-styled champion of the underdog. He talked about the Broadwater Farm trial. I said: 'They didn't stand a chance,' meaning all were guilty. He nodded, misunderstanding: 'The whole system's weighted against them. You can't just throw charges around without evidence. It's indecent.'

I told him about my latest idea for marketing cold remedies. He laughed. He laughed at everything I said. We swapped notes on the silly notices our mothers had in their kitchens: Although this house is quite a mess, Come in, relax, converse. It doesn't always look like this, Sometimes it's even worse!

Then he took my hand: 'Let's go somewhere else.'

So, because I didn't want to seem over-eager by dragging him home, we went to a club I knew in West Hampstead. He could barely drive, but we were on such a high. Each time we inadvertently touched, it was like being shot through with 240 volts. I was desperate to hold him.

We drank more and danced: Bon Jovi, 'Living on a Prayer'; Phyllis Nelson, 'Move Closer'. Then, somehow, his face brushed mine and we kissed. We couldn't stop. I asked him to come back and we both agreed to keep some clothes on so it wouldn't go too far.

He was wearing a dark blue shirt, brown loafers and dark socks. As soon as we got through the door we were on the floor. I remember looking at you lying there, Buster, as I undid your shirt and took over because I couldn't wait. I remember pushing your legs apart with my knee and kissing you all the way down through your navy trousers. And then we came over all coy and changed into T-shirts and slipped into bed and we played with each other till morning, without penetration.

It was the sexiest night of my life.

A man and his mate go into the pub. The man says to the barman: 'One pint for me and a brandy for the donkey.'

The barman turns to the mate and asks: 'Why does he call you donkey?'

The mate replies: 'I don't know. 'E aw, 'e aw, 'e always calls me that.'

It is nine o'clock. Maddie and Mala phone within minutes of each other. Buster has not come home. When he does, he will be drunk. I wait in the kitchen dreading the confrontation.

We got engaged. A silly notion, but it seemed so romantic. He'd proposed every day for six months. We talked about everything – even what type of schooling we wanted for our children. Buster said: 'We agree on everything. Our aspirations are identical. You know, Nina, we're perfectly matched.'
So we married the following September.

It is ten o'clock. Buster's mother calls. I have nothing to report. 'Don't worry,' she says. 'I'm quite sure this will sort itself out. I'm here if you need anything.'

In the third year of marriage, Lilla arrived. Jack followed when she was three and a half. We were ecstatic. We got a bigger house and Buster was made a partner. It meant longer hours but the rewards were immense. Then they changed the rules so solicitors could retrain as barristers. Buster started studying on the side. He had less time and was often tetchy. 'I never get a moment's peace to do my work.'
I became a full-time mother, running a home and networking within the community. I wrote the nursery newsletter. Now I asked my own mother to come and help in the evenings – to give us both a break from domestic routines. I learned about plants and painting. It was a bit like living out a Buffy Saint Marie song: except we didn't have the big brown dog.

*　　*　　*

It is eleven o'clock. Buster is due home shortly.

Six months ago, Buster started acting strangely. He became steadily more distracted. I've already mentioned the tarot cards and Radio One. He told me his priority was to become rich and famous. 'The family will have to take a back seat.'

He was frustrated that middle age was beckoning and those who'd been longer in the job were taking silk. Ah yes, I said to myself, a classic mid-life crisis. Isn't he sweet? I love him so much!

Woman in pub: 'Barman, I'll have a double entendre please.'
'Certainly madam would you like a big one?'

He began locking himself away to make phonecalls: even to his office. When I questioned him about the secrecy, he said he locked himself away because of the questions.

He stopped speaking to me and started arguing with Lilla and Jack. One night I found him on the landing with a distraught toddler screaming: 'I don't know why we ever had these *fucking kids*.' I thought he was having a breakdown.

I said a few times: 'Once the Keating trial is over, we need to take a break, just the two of us.' But I don't know if he was really listening.

I call Maddie: 'He's gone for a drink! He won't be home till late.'

She says: 'Pack him an overnight case and send him to his mum. Give him time out. He's probably drunk. If you talk now, you'll regret half of what you say.'

I go upstairs and pull out the brown kid bag he brought back from a trip to the Caribbean – something to do with a man on Death Row and an appeal to the Privy Council in England.

I pack his jeans and two clean shirts, his contact lens pot, lens fluid, razor and glasses. I write him a note: Buster, go to your mum's and think things over – she knows. We can talk tomorrow once the kids are in bed. Nina.

He won't go to his mum. He'll go to her. To Christine Brown. They'll make love three times. But right now I don't know that, and while I'm nearly at tomorrow, there's still midnight and the early hours, which are a sort of temporal limbo, to come.

Boss to secretary: 'Put this notice up on the clock, Miss Pym. I want to make sure everyone sees it.'

Time flies. You don't need to enjoy yourself. Once you get past twenty-five, it just flies anyway. You stop for ten minutes to take breath and when you look up it's like you've just exited the Twilight Zone. Years have gone by with barely a marking on the route.

Marriage is the ultimate Twilight Zone. Time passes through your fingers in a trickle of sand. Then, one day, you look down and realise it has you trapped up to the neck.

I never felt trapped with Buster. Well, no more than anyone else. But when he went, I looked down. All I could see was sand.

At midnight I go to sleep. No, not sleep: bed. I lie in the dark making out shapes on the ceiling.

At twenty past midnight, I hear Buster outside, fumbling for his key. He stumbles into the hall and straight over the overnight bag. The light goes on.

He seems slightly breathless as he reads my note. I sense a momentary hesitation. I yearn for him to come loping upstairs full of love: 'I'm so sorry, Nina. It's all a terrible mistake.' No, not Buster. He's a barrister: they don't make mistakes. Not that they admit to, anyway.

He goes through to the kitchen. I hear him pick up the phone. Calling a cab to the Goodholme-stead. I feel proud to have stepped back and allowed him time to think; I feel virtuous.

He pours himself a drink. He makes a second call. To her? Does he really think I'm asleep up here?

Today my world has been turned upside down.

I wonder who he *really* saw this evening.

Ten minutes later there's a gentle tap on the front door. Buster hurries into the hall and picks up the bag.

He shuts the door gently behind him.

I lie unmoving for fifteen minutes. Then I cry into the pillow and, miraculously, fall asleep.

PART TWO

TOMORROW

It's the excess above what you expect that makes
the force of the blow

∫

We meet in Pizza Express.

Buster orders garlic dough balls and an Americana, and then, without waiting, a Fiorentina for me. We know each other so well. I say: 'How are you?'

He says: 'I slept with Christine last night. At her sister's.'

It's like being kicked by your mother. I stare at him in wonder. Winded; wounded. He's puffed out; triumphal. I mutter, almost to myself: 'Then there's no going back.'

'I told you that.'

'Was it good?'

'We did it three times.' A big, boyish grin. 'How can you detect a vaginal orgasm?'

I say: 'If She'd a vaginal orgasm, Buster, She'd know.'

The dough balls arrive. I feel sick. Buster balances two between his thick fingers and swirls them in the garlic butter. It drips on his chin as he shovels them hungrily into his mouth.

I stare at my husband uncomprehendingly.

When love dies, so does memory. The past blurs. It is rewritten, re-evaluated, reshaped like a jug on the potter's wheel. Water is poured over the smooth furrows of the clay until it dissolves in an unfocused line; the mouth of the vessel, once wide and open, narrows into a spout;

the handle is wrenched off. Words of kindness, promises made; all these count for nothing. Here is our love, once solid and overflowing, refashioned as an ornament – an amusing knick-knack on the shelf of life.

Yesterday I was Buster's wife. Who am I today?

Women believe that, through marriage, we can change our men. In truth, we change ourselves.

Men fill the dishwasher and talk about load sharing. We do everything else and say nothing. Then friends visit and the husband dons an apron and does a Delia Smith; the wife beams with pride: look at my New Man!

I am that woman.

I am the woman who bore his children; who praised his successes and glossed over his mistakes. I am the woman who supported him through thick and thin, and who extracted enough pleasure from his presence to also support myself. I am the woman who continued to love him while he was falling in love with someone else.

I have shaped my life around Buster. Without him, who am I?

Buster cuts into his Americana. 'Christine told Peter this morning.'

'No children?'

'He fires blanks.'

I'm stunned by his bullishness. And my cow – ering. I say, stupidly: 'I hope you used protection.'

'I filled them with water to check they hadn't leaked.'

I hiss at him: 'So that *is* what it's all about. Sex.'

He rolls his eyes, and finishes his mouthful. 'It's not about sex, Nina. It won't happen again for a week – Christine doesn't do it during her periods.'

Bewildered, I watch him finish his lunch. He looks up, motioning at my plate: 'Not hungry?'

From my purse I pull out a photograph of Lilla and Jack

playing in the kitchen and force him to look at it. 'What about *them*, Buster: where do they come into this?'

'They'll get over it.' He sees my look. 'You're the one who said there's no going back!'

'I meant the damage was done, Buster. That would be harder to put right.'

He's exasperated. 'I'm doing what's right, Nina.'

This morning Maddie and Gavin came over. Gavin took our children to Saturday morning pictures. Maddie and I stood looking out at the garden. 'Your grass needs cutting.'

'It's too wet.'

'Too early in the year, too.' She craned her neck: 'You've got crocuses at the back. Lovely.' Without moving her gaze, she put her arm around my shoulder. 'You know I'm not very good at this sort of thing, Nina, but whatever you need, you only have to ask. I'm here for you. We both are.'

I started crying. Again. 'I know.'

She sighed: 'I've bought some chocolate eclairs from Maison Blanc. Let's start by comfort eating.'

Later, I will moan that I'm the only abandoned wife who stayed fat. I will lie in scented baths, enjoying the late-night silence and wonder how, in the years since meeting Buster, my figure went from hour glass to beer glass. From fit, to phut.

One night, out dancing, I'll meet a married man who boasts: 'You should have seen me ten years ago, I was so good-looking the women fell at my feet.'

When I concur that I too was lovelier ten years previously, he'll motion to our respective girths: 'If this is what marriage does to you, why do we bother?'

That's a hard one to answer.

Anyway, marriage doesn't do it to everyone: only the ones who're content in each other's company and sit together talking – putting the world to rights – across dinner.

And the ones slumped on the sofa watching *Coronation Street*.

And the ones who see friends three nights a week.

And the ones who have children.

And the ones who come home exhausted and go to bed.

And the ones who get drunk and fight.

And the ones who make love and then eat chips.

Thinking about it, maybe it *is* what marriage does to you.

I say to Buster: 'Do you want my pizza as well?'

He shakes his head.

I say: 'Buster, this is crazy. We've been so happy together. Why don't we get counselling?'

In three days' time we will have emergency counselling.

A kind-looking man in spectacles and anonymous clothes will sit on a black swivel chair and watch us tear each other apart in the civilised and understated vocabulary of the inept professional classes.

I express only half my feelings because I want Buster back. But he is the soldier whose strength is being sapped by a gangrenous leg that needs amputating.

He says: 'Nina's decision to marry me wasn't like Elizabeth Bennett with Mr Darcy, it was more like Emma . . . the arrangement of a suitable union.' He doesn't even know Emma's surname. Woodhouse. Or the name of her beau. Mr Knightly. He's never read Jane Austen. It's Christine's line.

The counsellor says: 'Why did you marry him, Nina?'

I think about it and then I say: 'I don't know.'

We are both reinventing the past as protection: Buster as a series of ill-portented beads strung into a necklace of misadventure. He conjures up long-forgotten events and exchanges and imbues them with sinister meaning. 'My ex-girlfriend gave us some trouble. Nina hated her. She wouldn't let me see or talk to her.'

And I, struggling to rationalise the present, become the victim: the woman who gave up everything for nothing. Hard-done-by; cheated. 'All I do is give. I'm raising two children full-time and earning money on the side by copy-editing. Buster expects me to be his muse, his lover, his mother, his best friend – and I'm tired.'

The counsellor barely moves. He says: 'I cannot see how you can go forward from this point. You both talk in absolutes.' What he *doesn't* say is: 'Buster, you've behaved like a prat. Go home and do the right thing.'

Maddie cut the ribbon and took two eclairs from the white cardboard box. 'Oh hell: these ones have a chocolate custard filling. I didn't notice.' She licked brown cream from her finger. 'You don't mind, do you?' I shook my head as she put them on to plates and sat down. 'Okay, Sis, what are we going to do?'

Sometimes, there's something we're desperate to get out of our systems: words, thoughts, emotions; but, no matter how we try, fate or inadequacy conspires to stop us.

It's like the man who takes his elderly father to check out a new nursing home.

As they're sitting on a sofa in the main aisleway, the old man starts tilting slowly to the left. A passing doctor bolsters him with pillows until he's upright. A few seconds later, the man starts tilting to the right. A nurse wanders across and piles several more pillows on the other side so he's again straightened. After a minute the old boy suddenly tips forward. Immediately an orderly rushes from a nearby office with cushions to correct the lean. The son turns round to his father and says: 'Well, Dad, don't you think this is a great place?'

'It's all right,' the old man replies. 'But I wish they'd let you fart in peace.'

Buster picks at my pizza crust.

I say: 'Buster, how are you going to afford a new life when we're all dependent on you? Lilla's fees are overdue.'

He says: 'Can't you sell your engagement ring?'

We chose the ring in Hatton Garden. It was a baking London summer; we both bunked off work and walked up towards Grays Inn before cutting east into the street of jewels. Every window was a variation on a theme. We were dazzled; delighted. In the end we chose a double ribbon of tiny diamonds and emeralds.

I wore it into work the next morning. One of the BCAF partners, Paul Avedon, saw me showing it off to the team. He said: 'You know emeralds are supposedly unlucky?'

'On what basis?'

He shrugged: 'The colour, I suppose. They say green cars are unlucky, don't they?'

'Did your wife have emeralds, Paul?'

He laughed. 'Yes. Don't say I didn't warn you, Nina.'

Paul Avedon and Lois Flaherty married in the Bahamas in the days when it wasn't an option in a Thomsons brochure. Their reception was at the Blue Elephant in Hammersmith. They sold their flat on Prince of Wales Drive and bought a five-bedroom semi in the Wandsworth toast rack – very chic even then. Lois wore Issey Miyake. They started a small ad agency together – Avedon Flaherty – and became phenomenally successful.

After three years they merged with Bugle Casey and became BCAF. They had his and hers offices next to each other and matching silver bangles with their names engraved. Her Porsche was blue; his black. They were the envy of the office.

But even the best marriages are fragile: for they depend on the constancy and consistency of the human heart and the human ego.

Lois was running a campaign for a major car company that had brought in one of Ferrari's top designers and was revamping the marque. She was invited on a three-day trial in the Dolomites: to give her a feel for the product. The designer was her guide. Over seventy-two hours, he gave her rides in the entire fleet: she was smitten. At the end of three days, she told Paul she was staying on for a long weekend and flew to Venice with a man who understood line and torque in a peculiarly Italianate way. After a night of love in a private apartment overlooking the Grand Canal, Lois decided to renounce the years of joy and partnership with Paul.

'It's not as if we have kids,' she was overheard crying in the boardroom one fraught morning.

Two days later she moved out.

Six weeks later the great romance was over. The designer himself was married with a number of children he'd neglected to mention – partly because he'd viewed their liaison as nothing more than client entertainment. So Lois limped back to SW17 with her Louis Vuitton luggage.

Paul had changed the locks.

I kissed my diamond and emerald ribbons. I said: 'Don't be so bloody superstitious, Paul. Trees are green, the grass is green, even petrol's green these days. It can't be that unlucky.'

He smiled and took my hand: 'I wish you and Buster all the luck in the world, Nina. Congratulations.'

A family of four comes into Pizza Express and is shown to an adjoining table. I think of all the times Buster and I have come here with Lilla and Jack and am overcome at the thought that we will never eat out as a family again.

Except of course we do, later: to tell the children that we are no longer a family. We take them to a restaurant in Soho and while they're tucking into sesame prawn toast we tell them that Mummy and Daddy are not getting on. That Buster will be staying somewhere else for a bit.

'How long is a bit?' Lilla asks.

He says: 'We've been arguing a lot. We'll have to see.'

I say: 'A long time, Lilla.' Because I already know.

'But Mummy and Daddy, you *never* argue.'

Buster says: 'That's because I've moved out.'

I say: 'Buster, I just heard the cock crow three times.'

Man to wife: 'The blokes down the pub reckon the milkman's screwed all but one of the women in this street.'

Wife: 'Really? Must be the sour cow at number forty-two.'

'Buster, do you love me?'

He meets my eye awkwardly: 'No.'

Death; inner death. 'When did you stop loving me?'

He shifts uncomfortably: 'I don't know, Nina. There's no particular moment that I can pinpoint.'

I say: 'Did you not love me before you fell in love with her?'

He shrugs: 'In my mind our marriage was over a long time ago.'

'If that's true, why didn't you tell me?'

'I tried to.'

'How did you try?'

He calls over the waitress and orders a coffee.

I say: 'Buster, however determined you are at this minute, you must know that life isn't that simple. That you can't just walk out of a door and assume that others will fill the cracks.'

He shrugs.

'Surely Christine must see how much the children need you. How can she live with this on her conscience?'

Buster frowns: 'Don't start criticising Christine. You don't know her.'

The other woman; the mistress; the doxy.

Mala's first husband, Jay, was a stuck-up author who, with her help, wrote skits on Thatcherite politics and the death of socialism. He and Buster were old schoolfriends. They spent happy evenings discussing politics and policy while Mala and I bonded over tiramisu and Tia Maria.

When Jay suddenly left Mala for another woman, Buster and I were bewildered. We chewed the fat and concluded he'd gone mad: especially when we learned Mala's rival was a bottle blonde in frumpy black who'd once been a hostess on *The Price is Right*. Buster said: 'I will never speak to him again.' And didn't.

Jay's doxy drove a Japanese car and answered phones in an Oxford police station. She gave him a tape – Lisa Stansfield, *Real Love*. He played it all the time despite the fact they had only one thing in common: Nicholas Parsons – who'd been present at a Foyles' literary lunch where Jay was guest speaker.

He said: 'Unlike you, she has time for me, Mala.'

Their children were then two and four and Mala was freelancing full time.

Jay's mistress massaged his ego, which had been deflated by the premature remaindering of his latest book. She perched on his knee and trawled hungrily through his intellectual card system, hearing everything and absorbing nothing.

'What does he see in her?' Mala wailed over pizzas at Orso's. 'She's exactly the sort of woman he used to poke fun at. Love really must be blind.'

Maddie, who was footing the bill in her capacity as moonlighting restaurant reviewer, shrugged: 'It isn't that love is blind. It's just that in times of emergency, it's indiscriminate.'

Later, when she starts peeling away the layers that lead to the heart of Christine Brown, Maddie will sniff: 'Buster was such a rigid man, Nina. Maybe he got confused by the chaos in your lives. Maybe he needed order.'

My sister and I are chalk and cheese. Her dolls from childhood were passed on to Lilla: unbroken and beautiful. All my mother recovered from my room was Mousetrap – with all the mice missing. Maddie is the anal retentive; I am the senna pod: same organ, different functions.

She has never understood the random phenomena in our house – the visiting kids, the problematic appliances, the constant ring of the phone, the vanishing remote control, the strange smell of gas near the front door. All of these have an underlying order. They present a unified whole known as family.

Maddie's children spend large amounts of time with their nanny, Susannah. Feeding times are taped on the fridge like a public information notice at the zoo, alongside a list of forbidden food additives. When they return from school, Charlie and Joe – IVF twins – are colouring and cutting, shaping and making, until teatime and bath.

At weekends, Maddie and Gavin put aside 'quality time' for the boys. He takes them to the park, she makes a traditional Sunday lunch and they sit around the table in the conservatory discussing *Power Rangers* intelligently.

It is not the same in my household – but she's wrong to think Buster couldn't deal with it. He loved the four of us sitting in bed on a Saturday night eating fish and chips and watching *Stars In Their Eyes*. It was fun.

Buster understood chaos theory: he understood how the neutrons and quarks of family life fitted together.

When he went to Christine, it wasn't because he could no longer stand the chaos at home. It was because he could no longer explain the chaos within him.

People deal with panic in different ways.

Three boy scouts, a lawyer, a priest, and a pilot are in a plane that is about to crash.

The pilot says 'We only have three parachutes, let's give them to the boys. They're young and have their whole lives in front of them.'

'Fuck the Boy Scouts!' shouts the lawyer.

'Do we have time?' asks the priest.

I watch Buster stirring his coffee. He is wearing the cobalt-blue Calvin Klein polo jumper I packed for him last night. It gives his cold eyes a real depth; a light. Like electricity is coursing through his irises. He meets my stare, waiting for me to say something. Challenging me to say something. I stay silent. The corners of his mouth tighten in an apologetic grimace.

Within a month of leaving, my husband the barrister will be wearing over-tight jeans, baggy jumpers and Hush Puppies. Sporting a Tony Blair haircut, he'll be zipping around town in a brand-new car and joining a gym where he'll rediscover his six pack abs and get a bit of lift on the chest area. But even now, twenty-four hours into this horror, I can no longer see into him. The gate has shut.

'Don't you think you're behaving strangely, Buster?'

'In what way?'

'In leaving a wife and family for a woman you've only been close to in a matter of weeks?'

'It may seem strange to you.'

'Yesterday, you were a husband and father. Today you're sleeping with someone else and never coming back.'

'There's no easy way of leaving, Nina.'

'But surely there are less cruel ways?'

'We – I – haven't thought about anything else.'

'Look Buster, I don't care that you've slept with her. I want you back. The three of us love you and need you.'

'You can't rationalise love.'

'You can rationalise anything you want. You used all the same phrases when you pursued me, Buster. You said you were out of control – you didn't leave me space to take a breath. I remember you losing the Jacobs case the morning after I refused to see you any more. You said you couldn't function without me. You phoned me every hour.'

In my mementoes box, I have a ten-page letter written by Buster during that time. 'My favourite fantasy, Nina, is of us in Waitrose with three trolleys of chocolate that we're taking home to bed.'

I'd refused to see him because, mistakenly, I thought he was dating someone else. Another Farters solicitor, Lesley. Later, I'd discover she was in the early stages of multiple sclerosis and he was helping her: advising on whether she should lighten her load or cover up. They'd had a couple of dinners together and, at one of them, he'd put his arm around her because she got upset.

I didn't know that then. All I knew was that Cathy, one of the BCAF trainees, had seen them in the Camden Brasserie and thought it best to tell me. I was young, brash and proud. That night, without explanation, I gave Buster his marching orders.

He called me at every opportunity. I slammed down the phone.

He cornered me outside BCAF. I told him to get lost.

He sent flowers.

At the end of the second week I agreed to meet him for dinner. He took me to the Camden Brasserie. I was mortified. He didn't once mention Lesley though I provided openings. At the end of the evening I said I would never see him again.

During the third week, Buster met Cathy at Chalk Farm station. She called him a bastard. Only then did the penny drop. He sent me the ten-page letter, two dozen roses and tickets for a weekend in Paris.

At the end of the fourth week we flew to Paris together. In a cheap hotel near Montmarte, we spent most of the time making love. There was horrible orange flowered wallpaper. I took a photograph of Buster naked, bending over the bed. It made us laugh. On the second night he held me to him so tightly I felt the breath going out of me. He said: 'Oh God, I love you. I've never felt like this about anyone before. It's crazy, it's irrational, and it's bloody fantastic. I love you, Nina.' He sang to me: Van Morrison, 'Crazy Love'. There were tears in his eyes. 'I can't believe it's possible to feel so much for one person. Please don't ever leave me again.'

The following week we bought the ring.

'All your relationships have followed a pattern, Buster. You proposed to me within days – you always get this way. The difference this time is you've got children. You can't just walk out on the basis that love is irrational.' I lean across the table so we're almost nose to nose over the bill: 'Do you remember holding Lilla at birth and saying that she was your number one – that you would do anything to make her happy? And Jack. You saw them first. You cut their umbilical cords.'

'I'm still their father. Living with someone else doesn't change that. Scars heal.'

I close my eyes and I see Lilla's trusting face and Jack,

strutting around, so confident in his own skin. And I cannot bear it.

A beautiful woman accosts an elderly man. 'Hey Buddy, would you like super sex?'

The old man thinks for a moment. 'I'll take the soup.'

Scars heal: but they're still scars. And the older you are, the longer the blemish stays on the skin.

Unlike birthmarks or skin disorders, scars have a story. A history. Each disfigurement represents a slip in the order of life. An unexpected attack which the body has beaten off.

A neighbour now recovering from throat cancer has two livid gashes from windpipe to ear; twenty years on, Mala's road protester friend, Beth, bears tracelines on her arm from junkie days; I still have gravel pits on my shin, where Lilla slipped and fell on me from the parallel bars in a children's playground.

Physical scars are visible reminders of endurance. Of survival. Of being healed. Of beating the odds.

They are the graffiti of everyday life: Kilroy was here.

But mental scars are problematic. They can't be inspected and rationalised while soaping yourself in the tub. They can't be prettified with a powder puff or turned into party pieces.

Mental scars, like the characters in *Scooby Doo*, hide behind doorways and shout 'Boo' when you least expect it.

Kilroy was here. And he never bloody left.

Buster pays the bill. Neither of us moves. The children have been taken out for the afternoon by his parents. They looked very old when they came to the door. His mother is one of my dearest friends. What the hell are we going to do?

*   *   *

This morning I said to Maddie: 'I feel more sorry for Buster than myself.'

'*Really?*'

'He's making the biggest mistake of his life.'

Dubiously she finished her eclair: 'He may have second thoughts.'

'If he'd had second thoughts, he'd never have gone.'

'I'm so angry I could scream. The man needs psychiatric help. I feel so useless, Nina. Why isn't there something we can do to make him realise what he's losing. What he's destroying?'

I carved a B into the fondant topping of my pastry. 'What I can't accept is the speed of it: how can a few months of passion wipe out nearly eleven years and two kids? Two days ago, I was happily married. I really thought Buster and I had got it right.'

She got up and filled the kettle. 'The bastard.'

I've already told you that when I married Buster, I told him that if he ever cheated on me, I'd cut off his bollocks and hang them on the gate. Just the thought of him with another woman made my stomach clench with anger in those days.

He'd say: 'Why are you even thinking things like this?'

I'd shrug: 'Women just do.'

After cutting off his bollocks, I was going to leave him, mutilated, to die slowly and painfully in a pool of blood on the kitchen floor. I don't know why I thought the kitchen and not a bedroom – maybe because it's easier to clean. All my life, major family gatherings have taken place around a kitchen table: my mother's; mine; Maddie's. Bidding Buster a bloody farewell on the blond ash while I stood sipping five-star Napoleon from a brandy glass, fitted with family tradition.

Then I was going to slip upstairs and destroy the things

he held most dear: his Boss suits, his Mac Powerbook, his Archbold, his ridiculous horsehair wig, his Anusol, his signed first edition of *Animal Farm*, his tennis racket, his Swiss army knife, his Daktarin and his yoga mat. Dear God, his yoga mat.

Even at this stage I know the one thing I will *not* miss about Buster is his daily pranayama – the gobbing yogic breathing exercises as he prepared to greet the sun – or whatever it is that yoga practitioners do. Lilla and I would watch and then we'd sing. Gaston's song from *Beauty and the Beast*: he's especially good at expectorating.

After the destruction of the artefacts that captured my husband's *Zeitgeist*, I planned to return for Buster's final moments. Moments when he would writhe in his own spume and beg – not for an ambulance, but forgiveness. My forgiveness. He would beseech me for absolution before the meeting with his maker. And I would laugh.

Then, when his various bits had been cleared away and I, somehow, had escaped prosecution on the grounds that Buster deserved it, I was going to go out.

Out to get rat arsed, paint the town red and bed every man under the age of thirty with a penis large enough to fill the Blackwall Tunnel.

I say to Buster: 'Shall we go for a drive?'
'Where?'
'I don't know. Maybe up the M1? I could do with clearing my head, couldn't you?'
He looks at me quizzically. 'Sure.'

It was partly my car he fell in love with. All the guys did.

I had a 1963 Carmen Ghia. It cost a fortune to keep on the road but it looked great. Anyway, I was a hot property at BCAF and they kept upping my money. Taking a man out in it was like riding a motorised love seat: hot, fast, juicy. If you just turned towards each other, you were within kissing breath.

I put in a brilliant new stereo system. The first in-car album I played was the Pet Shop Boys' *Actually*. Buster and I wound down the windows and flew through Hampstead blasting the town: 'It's A Sin'.

Now we own a family car. It has impressive lines, but it's boring. I said: 'Buster, can't we buy something a little zippier?'

He said: 'I'm a Legal Aid barrister – I don't earn enough.' He hugged me to him: 'Sweetheart, I'd buy you a Rolls-Royce if we could afford it, but we can't.'

Even now I yearn for an MGB or a Z3 or an XK8, but it will be Buster who, a few weeks on, buys himself a zippy new car.

How times change.

And how we change.

Who am I?

Overnight I have acquired a new persona. What is my job description now? What is my role now? Where will I find the old Nina – or the new one – amongst all the emotional grist being put through my mill? And if I *can't* find her, how can I guarantee getting through this?

I'm like the little boy who finds a green welder's mask in the road. Pulling it on, he excitedly goes in search of his mates.

As he turns the corner, a man slows down in his car: 'Hey, little boy – do you know what a French kiss is?'

'No Mister, I don't.'

'Do you know what a wank is?'

'No Mister, I don't.'

'Do you know what a blow job is?'

'No Mister, I don't.'

'Well now little boy, how about a fuck?'

The little boy throws his hands up in the air and starts to cry: 'Listen Mister, I don't know the answers. You see, I'm not *really* a welder – I just found this mask in the road.'

Maddie poured the tea. She said: 'You're not going to lose this house – d'you understand?' I shrugged. 'This is your home, Nina. It's where the children are secure and happy. He can't touch it. He *won't* touch it.' She wiped down the work surface with an old J-Cloth: 'What you need is a good solicitor. Don't you have any Microban?' I shook my head. 'I'll get you some. Not a local firm – they probably all know Buster. Bastard. I'll ask Gavin if he can recommend someone. He's not going to get you out of here.'

'I doubt he'll even try.'

'He'll change.'

I drank the tea: thick, sweet, comforting. I said: 'Buster's always put the kids first.'

'Really? Is that why he went?' She reached out and touched my hand: 'I'm sorry. I don't understand how you're so calm.' She smiled: 'You know me, I always want a solution. I don't like grey areas.'

I wailed: 'Why didn't he tell me? We could have changed things; rethought the way we live our lives. Worked harder at it.'

'You haven't done anything wrong, Nina. You're loyal and loving, you're a great mother, you pull your weight. It's Buster that's got a problem, not you.'

Later I'll watch a man talking about his own marriage break-up on TV. He says: 'I felt like I'd been standing on a precipice for a long time. I didn't know how or why I'd arrived there, but as soon as I met the other woman, I felt I could jump and she would catch me. It was a solution.'

'What did it feel like when you jumped?'

He smiles: 'It felt great. It felt fantastic. I wasn't in freefall,

I was dropping gently by degrees. Even though I wasn't happy, I was so at peace. It made perfect sense. It was my release from all that fear.'

'And did it last?'

'No.' He laughs humourlessly. 'Two years later I found myself lying face down on the ground. I woke up and realised what I'd done to the people who loved me the most. It was the most horrific day of my life.'

In the car Buster is ablaze. He is a man in love. Well, certainly in lust. In fatuated. He says: 'Don't you see that *you* have played a part in what's happened? If I was truly happy, I would never have fallen in love with someone else.'

I say: 'Breaking up your family is not the normal way of passing on that message.'

He laughs: 'I told you so many times. You were never interested in my work, Nina. Those months when I was working with Rock Marston on the Irish appeals, I'd be stressed and angry and you'd just tell me to pull myself together and stop whining.'

'Because you were driving us all crazy! You came home night after night with the same catalogue of complaints. You were like a dog chasing its own tail.'

I think back to the endless period when Buster was working with Rock, an up-and-coming media solicitor whose firm had secured all the Irish mis-trial appeals. Buster knew the points of law and he was the man who'd make the winning arguments, but propriety dictated Rock did the talking. In the months of pre-hearing talks and statements, Buster hated the fact that his part was never acknowledged.

I say: 'When I told you to pull yourself together, it wasn't because I wasn't interested, it was because there was nothing I could do to change things. Is that really the cause of your unhappiness?'

He looks nonplussed. 'Yes,' he says. 'Anyway, that was what started it.'

We go round the Staples Corner roundabout and on to the M1 motorway. It's a January Saturday: cold; empty. I say: 'How far shall we go?'

'Milton Keynes?'

As we drive, I talk about love in an abstract way so Buster won't get jumpy. I tell Buster what love means to me; what he means to me. How I'd envisaged us growing old together, still talking and laughing – doing things with our children and grandchildren. I say: 'Do you realise that if you go, we've just spent our last Christmas together as a family?'

Buster cannot apply himself to us; he is too caught up in the present: in Christine. He tells me again that her husband is a real bastard. 'You know he had an affair two years ago?' How would I know? Buster shakes his head regretfully: 'You wouldn't believe the way he's treated her.'

While Maddie was working off steam, Mala rang.

She said: 'What happened last night?'

'He came, got his bag and went to his mother's.'

'Are you alone?'

'No. Maddie's here. She's cleaning my fridge.'

'She's doing what? For God's sake! Where are the kids?'

'Gavin's taken them to Saturday morning flicks.'

'Has Buster called?'

'We're meeting for a late lunch.'

'Don't reason with him, Nina. Just tell him to get the fuck back.'

I say: 'Buster, come back home.' He slumps in the passenger seat as if about to fall asleep. I say: 'Listen, Buster, twenty-four hours ago you hadn't even slept with this woman. Now she's the centre of your life. If she's so bloody great, how come she got involved with a married father of two?' He turns his face away. I shout: 'Look at me!' I put my hand on my heart and the car swerves. 'You're talking about her as if she's your future. She isn't. *I'm* your future. Lilla and Jack are your future. We'll work on this together. Stop all the shitting about and come home. This isn't a multiple choice option.'

'I'm not "shitting" about. Christine *is* my future.'

'What about her husband?'

'Maybe the two of you should get together?' Buster says.

There *are* situations where men and women swap both partners and families. I've read about them in the *News of the World* and the *National Enquirer*. It happens. But not a lot.

The last thing I wanted when Buster left, was Christine's husband.

I wanted Christine to want her husband.

The absent-minded professor is working in his study.

His wife pops her head round the door: 'Hertz, do you realise it was thirty years ago today that you proposed to me?'

'And did you accept?'

Mala says that marriage shouldn't be a life sentence.

She says this because she's always being released on probation.

I argue: 'Perhaps marriage *should* be a life sentence – that's the ultimate security isn't it?' When she doesn't respond, I say: 'What about your *children*, Mala? What signals are they getting on the nature of love?'

A shrug: 'At the end of the day, modern women have few options. The best we can do is teach our children to be strong. I don't want love to be the be all and end all for them. Times have changed. There's more to life than coupling, Nina.'

*   *   *

Within days of Buster leaving, I will start looking at men in a way that I haven't for years: an animal way. Like a wounded creature seeking a new mate, I will find myself reassessing the characteristics and status of every man who crosses my path. It is as if a veil has been lifted from before me.

The wedding veil has been lifted from before me: and mine eyes can see unto the hills.

Every morning the children come in at six.

Until the day Buster went, this was our routine:

Lie awake, complaining, until seven. Go downstairs. He: makes coffee, empties dishwasher, brings in the papers and gets breakfast for the household. She: finds clothes, makes packed lunches, wipes down and dresses children.

Eight thirty: children ready and restless. Buster still reading news or court papers with his cab outside. Panic.

Eight forty. She: chivvies children into car. Lilla dropped off eight fifty-five Jack in nursery by ten past nine. He: showers, grabs briefcase and takes cab, either to court or to chambers off Grays Inn Road.

Nine thirty: I return, clear up, and copy-edit for a publisher until Jack is dropped back at twelve fifteen. I make his pasta and we talk and play until he's ready to sit down and watch *Tot's TV*.

Here I catch up with the papers and any outstanding reading. I sort out laundry/shopping/cleaning and at three we get Lilla. Some days she does a class – tennis or art – but most days we have other children back for tea.

At five, I cook a dinner, feed the kids, put away dressing-up clothes left on the floor, wipe wet paint off the kitchen table, entertain collecting parents and trip over the dice, dominoes and chequers that are lying around where Jack, yet again, has upended the compendium of games.

By the time Buster came home, the children were in the bath and I was desperate for relief. I'd listen to them laughing fighting for his attention over stories and tapes and be glad I was downstairs.

I cleared up the remaining debris and waited for him to join me. It was lovely to have adult company. His company.

I turn the car round at Milton Keynes.

I say: 'Buster, doesn't the fact that you and I can talk so candidly about what's happened say more about the nature of our relationship than any of the misgivings that propelled you into another woman's arms?'

'What do you mean?'

'Well, we've talked about how many times you fucked; about vaginal orgasms; about Christine not doing it during a period. These aren't the normal things a man tells his wife.' He doesn't respond. 'I'm your best friend, Buster. You're sharing everything with me because you know I love you. Don't you see that our friendship alone is worth more than what Christine gives you?'

'I hope we'll always be friends, Nina.'

'You're missing the point, Buster.'

'I'll always think of you as my friend.'

Somehow I stay calm. I say: 'Buster, if you don't come back, we can never be friends. This isn't how friends behave towards each other. I asked you yesterday to give me three months. *Three months* to try and change things; three months to at least acclimatise the children. If that doesn't work, go with my blessing and we *can* be friends. If you don't, we can never get past that.'

Friends are people who forgive transgressions; who remain loyal through thick and thin.

Like the Morris Minor filled with ancient crones. Pulling

them over for driving too slowly on the motorway, the policeman says: 'Madam, don't you know that going under the limit is just as dangerous as exceeding it?'

The driver, elderly and confused, responds: 'Officer, I don't understand. I was following the limit. Look at that sign – twenty-five miles an hour.'

The officer rolls his eyes disbelievingly: 'That's the route number, Madam, not the speed limit!' As the woman, clearly embarrassed, drops her head, he notices her wizened passengers are wide-eyed and white as sheets. Peering in the back he asks: 'Are your passengers all right?'

'Oh, they'll be fine, Officer. We've just come off the one two nine.'

Outside our home, Mala is my closest friend. We gelled as soon as we met. I tell her many things I wouldn't share with others: but nothing that I haven't shared with Buster.

This isn't to say that I tell Buster the same things I tell Mala. Often he gets just the bones of a story while I save the flesh for her. This is because Buster, like many men, only focuses on the big picture, and Mala, like most women, is curious about each brushstroke.

Women approach life scientifically. They enjoy dismantling relationships and situations and rebuilding them to see how the component parts were originally fitted together. If, it seems to them, the structure is basically unsound, they will attempt to reconstitute the flawed pieces in order to strengthen the original foundations. They are the engineers who test and service the nuts and bolts that hold communities together. They weld the cracks.

And men? Perhaps they approach life creatively. If they can't fashion something out of the pieces life hands them, they just chuck them on the floor and move to the next activity table. Which is why I would have tried to save our marriage; but Buster walked away without a backwards glance.

It is this divergence in the male and female approach to confidences that determines how we present them to the people in our lives. To our husbands, to our wives, to our best friends.

Except, Buster *was* my best friend. We'd sit in the bath together for hours, talking about life. You can't get much closer than that.

'How can you tell this isn't just lust, Buster?'

'We saw each other for four months without having sex.'

'*Just* for lunch?'

'Yes. I told you. It started as a friendship. We'd just talk. It wasn't planned this way.'

'Then why did you let it progress?'

'She understands what I do.'

'So do a lot of the *men* you deal with. Christine is only singled out by the dampness between her legs.'

'Don't talk about her like that.'

'When you worked with Christine on the Sendak case three years ago – that time I met her at the Christmas drink – you said she was neurotic. She drove you crazy because she was always having headaches and being dramatic.'

'She's careful about her well-being. You won't turn me against Christine, Nina. You don't know her.'

'What's important, Buster, is whether *you* know her.'

Two months after Buster has gone, an old friend sends a note: 'I can't believe that Buster of all people could do this. It just shows you can never know anyone completely.

'Take heart, Nina, you will get past this. You have suffered a bereavement. The man you once knew is dead – as is the future as you saw it. Don't be afraid to talk, cry or scream: and know we are all talking, crying and screaming with you.'

The death of my future as I saw it. Nina and Buster, Lilla and Jack. Big house with garden; holidays in the sun; Sundays together in the big bed; evenings shared with good friends; fun; love; laughter; lust; lolling.

And they all lived happily ever after.

Buster and I married within eighteen months of meeting. I wore pale grey and lavender: a flamenco-style dress with a bolero jacket run up by a woman in Chelsea. It set off my olive colouring and dark hair – blue-black that year. We pulled it up and stuck a large orchid on top: very stylish. We arrived at the church in a red, fintailed fifties Cadillac. Buster's secretary, an amateur opera singer, performed the Ave Maria from the church gallery. We both cried. Outside, the gang from my office made an arch of gladioli – inspired by a campaign for the Australian tourist industry. It was a wet but wonderful September day. Everyone was laughing.

But it wasn't until much later that I discovered Buster had once been a Young Communist; a county swimming champion; Hamlet in a university production. It was only when I started to organise Lilla's christening I discovered his almost pathological hatred of organised religion. 'I did the wedding for you, Nina: that's enough. The imposition of mythical standards and absolutes. Crap.'

I didn't know any of these things about Buster, before.

Then, one day, after years of forging a reputation as a committed defender of the wronged, he agreed to represent a known multiple rapist. I said: 'How could you, Buster?'

He said: 'It's the cab rank principle – first come, first served. I don't have a choice in these things, Nina.'

But we both knew he did.

So much new information about someone I already knew so well.

How much can he possibly have learned about Christine in four months of occasional, longing, lunches?

So often we make sweeping assumptions about other people when we're barely able to recognise ourselves.

A confused old man arrives at the gates of Heaven. St Peter says: 'Who are you?'

The old man sighs: 'I don't remember.'

'Surely there's some clue in your past?'

A shake of the head: 'All I know is that I was a carpenter, and my son was very famous.'

St Peter frowns. 'What else?'

'That's it. I had a wood workshop. I was a nobody. But he – from the moment he was born, he was special. Everyone in the world knew him. They loved him. They called out his name.'

St Peter wipes his brow. 'Stay here.' He goes running across the clouds: 'JC, JC, come quickly. There's a man at the gates who I think is your dad.'

Jesus rushes to the entrance, his arms outstretched. 'Father?'

Suddenly the old man's face breaks into a smile of pure pleasure: 'Pinnochio?'

I say: 'What are you going to do now, Buster?'

'I'll stay with my parents for a bit.'

'Until the two of you get a flat around the corner?'

'I don't know.'

'You don't know very much for someone who's just destroyed his family.'

'You're always so melodramatic, Nina.'

My eyes mist over as I slow down for the Staples Corner roundabout. I turn on the radio.

All Saints, 'Never Ever'. I need to know what I've done wrong; and how long it's been going on.

We are at the end of the M1. I say: 'One day, Buster, you will look back at what you've done, and how you've done it, and you will hate yourself.'

It is the end of our journey: literally and figuratively. The M1 has been my road to Damascus. I drive home, alone.

Home is two miles from the motorway. A Victorian terraced house in the middle of a community dominated by thirty somethings. I know every child in the street: every car; every dog; every lead-light front door. Home is not just where the heart *is*: it is the manifestation of the heart – of love and longing and romance. The bike in the hall; the missing bathroom tile; the tin of Slimfast; the family montage on the fridge. All of these indicate who we are and where we come from; the essence of our lives.

I open the red door and enter the empty house. I stand looking at myself in the hall mirror. My grandfather's mirror. Little spots of mercury have started showing through, catching the light; twinkling like fading stars. I watch with almost detached interest as my face crumples and tears start coursing down my cheeks, so heavy my shirt is wet. I sit on the stairs and I bellow. I scream: 'WHY?' My sobs are so loud they bounce off the ceiling and echo around me. WHY?

I dry my face and call my in-laws. We have a chat. Kate is devastated. I try to put a smile in my voice.

Our families shape us. Even if we despise everything they represent, we do so as a direct result of having shared their environment and lived that experience.

Our families are our physical and psychological luggage.

From my first meeting with Buster's family, I was smitten.

They were a representation of everything I held dear: love, fidelity, warmth, security. In luggage terms, they were top-of-the-range Samsonite. I admired the strength of their curves; the versatility of their compartments; the way the different shapes, sizes and functions complemented each other. I bought the set.

Maddie said: 'You're so lucky. Being around Gavin's parents is like waiting for dough to rise.'

In the Goodholme house, I sit and read the papers while the kids climb over Buster's parents or raid the dressing-up box, coming back as Chinese ladies and top-hatted magicians. We chat around the big dining table, swapping stories and jokes. It's like going back in time to how families used to be. Happy.

Will Kate and Oliver Goodholme like my replacement?

Already I am thinking through the permutations. At some point, will She enter their home and sit next to their son at that same dining table; in the chair I have used for ten years? Will She cuddle up to him on the pink sofa, as we did virtually all our married life?

Will Buster want me in his childhood home? A reminder not only of what he rejected, but, as realisation slowly seeps into his testoronic pores, of what he's *lost*? Oh the guilt; the regret; the shame.

What will that do to a man like Buster who enjoys the social status that successful barristers confer on themselves?

I sit in a huddle making hopeful small talk with Kate; a GP; a Godsend when, suffering from parental paranoia, one mistakes prickly heat for German measles.

Oliver was once a mandarin in the Foreign Office. When he was restructuring the Hong Kong civil service. Buster and I flew out to stay at his huge apartment in Sha Tin. I was pregnant with Lilla. We shopped by day and ate out in car parks that transformed after dark into makeshift restaurants. Buster had three suits made, including a tuxedo. I bought four silk blouses that still hang unworn in my wardrobe.

A couple of times, we jumped the jetfoil to Macau; we ate giant prawns and blew money in the casinos. We had a day in Canton, watching in amazement as Chinese housewives carried home that evening's dinner, still breathing. Ducks, their heads peering over the tops of plastic carrier bags; dozens of frogs impaled on iron skewers, writhing in a slow dance of death.

'Only eat vegetables,' Buster warned. 'We don't want strange bestial juices travelling down into baby Goodholme.'

On the mainland, we often stayed out till breakfast time, dancing in the frenetic clubs of Lan Kwai Fong. It was a second honeymoon. On our last night, his father took us for dinner at the Peninsular Hotel. 'I'm so very glad that Buster married you, Nina,' he said. 'You complement each other so well.'

Who am I now?

A pleasant woman with whom their son had children.

Maddie and Gavin return Lilla and Jack who run past me giggling. I say my goodbyes at the front door. Maddie says: 'Have you told Mum yet?'

'It'll break her heart.'

'Shall I do it for you?'

'No. Let's wait until it's all a bit clearer.'

'You need her.' I shake my head. 'And you need me. I'll stay.'

I try to smile. 'We're survivors, Mads; you know that. I'll be fine. I need to think. You've done enough, anyway. Let me be for a while.'

Mala calls. She says: 'I've got babysitting. Don't argue. I'm coming over.'

Lilla, washed and scented in a Barbie nightie, starts pulling at me while we're talking. Suddenly angry, I hit her across the head and scream: 'Why can't you just leave me alone?' She starts to cry.

Mala says: 'Take it easy, Nina. You're all they've got now.'

I give the children Phenergen to knock them out. I put on bedtime tapes for them. I sit on the toilet and weep. Lilla calls for me. I wipe my face and go to her. She looks at me curiously: 'What's made you unhappy, Mummy?'

I say: 'Grown up things. Silly things.'

'I'm sorry I was rude.'

'That's all right, Sweetheart.'

She catches a renegade tear with her stubby little fingers: 'Are you crying because you're sad or because you've hurt yourself?'

'Because I'm hurting, Sweetheart.'

'Shall I kiss you better?'

I smile at her: 'I wish you could, but the hurt's inside.'

Mala has brought a half bottle of vodka with her: 'I didn't have any cash so I raided the drinks cupboard and found this. Have you got mixers?' She pulls two *Pocahontas* beakers from the cupboard and mixes large quantities of spirit with the dregs of the breakfast Tropicana. 'Here's to the forging of new habits.' It tastes terrible; too strong. I down it in one. 'Feel better?' I shake my head. She smiles: 'Don't worry, you will. Just give it a minute or two.'

Old habits die hard. New habits don't replace them, they co-exist alongside. I think of Sam and Harry the two rabbits who, after months of planning, escape from an animal testing laboratory by burrowing through their hutches and jumping the wall at midnight.

At daybreak they find themselves in a field full of the

juiciest carrots ever seen. By early evening their little tummies are like footballs. They fall asleep happily in the thick green grass.

When they wake, the first thing they notice is hundreds of lady rabbits in the adjoining field – all making goo-goo eyes at them. Excitedly the boys bound across. After several hours making rabbit love, they pass out, exhausted, under a tree.

In the morning, Sam gets up and says: 'I'm sorry, Harry, but I'm going back to the lab.'

'Back to the lab? Are you crazy? We've got endless carrots, and totty on tap. What on earth are you going back for?'

Sam shakes his head sadly. 'I can't help it, mate: I'm just dying for a fag.'

All feeling is relative. In recent times I've often felt fed up with Buster. He didn't leave enough time in the day for the children and me. He pratted around taking up yogic postures. He was bad tempered and dismissive. Particularly towards the end; when she was in his blood. But I told you about that, yesterday.

I thought: if our lives carry on like this, I'm not sure how long I can stand it. What I meant was: *things must change*.

At that time, I would have felt better if Buster had just sat down, held my hand, and told me he loved me. I would have passed off his surliness as a standard bad patch.

Yesterday, I would have felt better if Buster had sat down, held my hand, told me that he loved me, and agreed to try and save our marriage before walking out.

This afternoon, I would have felt better if Buster had sat down, held my hand, and told me that he still had *some* love for me. Some love, somewhere; anywhere.

But he hasn't left me because of a bad patch. He's left me because of a wet patch.

Now I can only feel better if I get drunk and obliterate the last thirty-six hours from my memory banks. At least, that's what Mala says.

I lie in bed and wonder how my world has changed so completely in twenty-four hours. Yesterday morning I was a happily married woman with a bad tempered husband. We had two beautiful children, a lovely home, and a future stretching ahead full of promise.

Yet it became the saddest day of my life. What does that make today? Perhaps it is the maddest day of my life.

I have discussed my partner's infidelity with Christine Brown in lurid detail over a pizza.

I have been told by the man around whom I built my life, that he does not love me.

I have stood helplessly by as the template of our future was picked up and dashed against a wall.

I lie in the dark repeating like a mantra: what happens now? My mind is full of crude, cruel, thoughts. We have been felled by a blow from my husband's probondis; our lives fluttering in rags from his pork sword.

I rock myself silently, a family and its shared history consigned to the dung heap by the lure of some sad sow's sliver of rancid cunt.

I ask myself how I will manage. Will he give me money? Will he force us to sell the house? In the adjoining rooms, Jack and Lilla are sleeping peacefully, unaware that the mainstay of our lives has removed himself. He says our children are resilient: what he means is they won't grow up to slit their wrists or become serial rapists. That they'll come to terms with the insecurity and sense of rejection; that by the time they're our age and going through divorces of their own, they'll recognise the pattern of failure that their parents have gifted to them.

Oh Buster. How could you?

PART THREE

LATER

Sod this for a game of soldiers, let's party

∫

I am lying in the dark in a Docklands studio with a man who is not my husband. Banks of electronic equipment line one wall, neon green zeroes from unset clocks flashing dementedly in the gloom. A World Cup fixture list is pinned to the door. Designer shirts are drip-drying on a rail by the window, the handles of an exercise bike silhouetted behind them.

Out of my line of vision, a row of unwashed cups line the kitchen worktops. Minutes earlier, when I went to make tea, my companion shouted: 'Don't drink from them unless you've scrubbed with Fairy.' The aluminium pans, bizarrely, are being soaked in bleach.

Going to the toilet, I sit awkwardly in the dark and the seat falls on to the floor with me still on it. 'You pay £200 a week to live in this place?'

A grunt in response.

Outside, just yards away, the Docklands Light Railway has started. I sit in the bed and look across at this sweet, unrealising, man.

It's five o'clock on a Saturday morning in mid-May.

I have lost my post-marital virginity.

We went out for dinner: Vic Naylors in Clerkenwell. I don't remember what we ate or said. I was thinking about the nicotine patch on his back; wondering what he looked like under the ochre YSL shirt. I was wondering what would happen when we kissed. Fourth date. He wanted pudding. I watched in disbelief as he wolfed it down.

Afterwards I dropped him back. He asked me in. The first time. I sat on the bench at the end of the bed drinking coffee. He sat next to me. The kiss was sudden and explosive. Not like kissing Buster. Not questing or questioning. Pure hunger.

Before we did it, when we were hot and his hands were edging under my shirt, I said: 'The last time I slept with a man who wasn't my husband, was ten years, thirty pounds and two children ago. I may chicken out.' He kissed me, again. New-old tremors; like standing high and looking down, knowing you can fall. He whispered: 'All you have to say is "stop", and I will.' So of course, I never said it. I just squeaked: 'Turn the lights off Nick, I don't want you to see me.' And as he came back, arms outspread, it was me who rolled him over, unzipped his trousers and started the show.

Deep deep kisses. Clothes coming off in bursts. At times I didn't even hold my stomach in. I had forgotten the pure smell of a man. New hands in old places. Too fast, too slow: yes, just like that. So strange; so wonderful. Suddenly such pressure in a private place; bodies taking over the detail. I said: 'Don't use a condom. Please.'

'I'm not ready for babies.'

'It's my safe time.'

And then he was inside me. And it was so different from before that the past was obliterated in one simple act.

When I look at the man who was Buster, I no longer recognise him. I have so many happy memories: of cuddles and laughter, gossip and jokes, the endless ideas that filled his mind; but I do not associate them with the man who comes to my door. Perhaps now, all that light and energy is rechannelled into Christine. Perhaps that is why I see only shadow.

Shadow as he gives me that boyish smile, gazing at me fondly over the heads of our children. As if the past months have not happened, and he is waiting for me to pull on my coat so we can all go to the park together. To push the kids on the swings, to get sand in our shoes, to drink hot chocolate in the watery sunshine.

So many times, other parents we knew would join us – Laura, Alan and the boys pushing bikes across to the café and stopping to put the world to rights over carrot cake and hot chocolate. It was all so commonplace and innocent. And happy. And cosy.

Too cosy perhaps for a man who set his path by the stars.

We were in The Engineer when Nick came up to me. It was the three-month anniversary of Buster's leaving. My old schoolfriend Liz had dragged me out. She said: 'I know it's a Monday night but why not? Get your mum in and we can have a gossip.'

Nick was with a work party. He kept looking at me across the room. When I went to the bar he approached. 'Celebrating?'

'I've just filed for divorce.'

'Shouldn't you be broken hearted?'

'What's the point?'

He shrugged: 'I don't know.'

His glance took in my left hand. No rings: thrown from a moving car the day Buster and I told the children the truth about Christine, and Lilla said: 'Daddy must love her more than us, or he wouldn't go, would he?'

Nick said: 'Does that mean that, technically, you're single?'

My stomach turned. 'I suppose it does.'

'Then let's share a drink.' Just like that.

In the half-light, I watch him breathing. This smooth-skinned man who has brought me into the real world where we arrive and leave alone. I pull the navy duvet with the diagonal flashes up to my neck, and lie against him back to back. I am filled with wonder at his presence; at the pure joy of sleeping with someone new. Which, somehow, is a much greater leap of trust than simply making love.

I roll over and press my soft body into his hard one. Spoons.

On the floor is a crumpled Chelsea flag. There are three different alarm clocks on the bedside shelf unit. Little air fresheners stand like sentinels above eye level. A copy of *The Economist* is thrown carelessly on one side. He's something in the City; coffee futures.

Another train hurtles past somewhere beyond the windows.

Groaning, I wonder how anyone can sleep through this.

Deep sleep is a gift lost to those with children. Semi-permanently, I have heavy-lidded Salman Rushdie eyes.

Not so, Buster. He wakes with Christine now. There are no cries in the middle of the night demanding his attendance. No six o'clock wakes-ups day in day out. No rushing around making Ready Brek and packed lunches, checking homework and dressing two small children. Did he really help with all that? Yes he did. He complained, like all parents; but he did all those things and more. Now he is reinvented. Reinvented as a completely rested being.

So why does he look so wretched?

'Do I look very old to you, Nick?'

'You look great, Nina.'
'But old?'
'No, at most you look the same age as me.' Thirty-two.

For the first weeks I hated the sight of myself.

I was old. Careworn. A domestic facilitator wanted by no one. Not even my husband. No Valentine's card; no kiss good night. I searched my own features for some clue to the person inside. My mother said: 'Nina, for what are you inspecting yourself?'

'I don't know. Signs of life?'

'Darling, you can't carry this disaster around your neck like an albatross. You have to shoulder it. We all have to do that in life.'

My mother, like Maddie, like me, is very practical. Two months after our father's funeral, she sat us down at the kitchen table. She said: 'We're on our own now girls. Your daddy wasn't a rich man, but we have our home and we're going to survive. Better than that: we're going to prosper. We are a trinity of women.'

A trinity of women. A Holy Trinity.

Religion sustains my mother. She tells me we're all God's children. I say: 'If we're all God's children, why doesn't he pay maintenance?'

Nick is scrubbing out the cups. 'The milk's gone green.'

I smile seductively. He hands me a hot drink. I wait for him to pounce. He says: 'Football training in half an hour.'

I sit in the morning gloom wondering how to move from bed to bathroom without exposing myself. He starts packing his kit into a red sports bag.

I say: 'Do you want me to go?'

He's surprised. 'Not before I do. Why?'

'I'm feeling surplus to requirements.'

'You're just oversensitive.'
'That's because I don't understand the rules of the game.'
'Of soccer?'
'Of dating.'

Mala gallops into the bar and virtually shouts: 'You've done
it then?' Struggling out of a Donna Karan mac, she orders
vodkas and grins at me: 'Feeling guilty?' I shake my head.
'It's funny how sex is such a big thing in our minds when
all it boils down to is exercise between consenting adults.'
'Is that what it is?'
'Yes. Was it momentous?'
I pull the slice of lime from my glass and suck on it. 'Yes,
it was momentous. Like the first time ever.'

I slip discreetly into the loo, clothes in hand. I lean naked
against the door looking down at myself.
Before babies, my boobs were the only part of me that
faced the magnetic pole. Now they'd miss the bull's eye.
But they're okay.
I straighten my shoulders and wonder if *he* noticed. I pull
in my stomach but the pouch of fat still sags there like a
Whoopee Cushion grafted on.
Nick said: 'You're a woman, Nina – this is how they are.'
Thighs like tugboats. Neatly polished toenails.
I rub Colgate round my gums with a finger. In the tube-lit
gloom I appear in soft focus in the bathroom glass. Tousled,
flushed; youthful. Outside, Nick has turned on the radio.
You can brush my hair, undress me everywhere. Aqua:
'Barbie Girl'.
I feel so wonderfully young; so alive.

Mala says: 'Do you remember the first time ever?'
'Of course. His name was Robbie. Robbie Valliant.'
Black hair, dark eyes, a Leo. Lived in Clapton; drove

a daytona-yellow Ford Mexico with Wolfrace dish mag wheels, a whiplash aerial and a Starsky and Hutch stripe. 'We played records in his room: Steven Stills, Tim Buckley, Joni Mitchell, the Allman Brothers. Endless stairs. Everything was painted black; even the ceiling.' There were Mucha posters on all the walls. He had a Goldring record deck and Wharfdale speakers. He rolled a joint. We lay down in front of the two-bar electric fire. On a decrepit goatskin rug. 'He was twenty; it seemed so old.' Brown velvet trousers – I remember those. 'God, I loved him.'

'Was it worth the wait?'

I say: 'Yes. We both knew the time was right.'

But we didn't know how. Undressed in the half dark, we were inelegant; inexpert. I was rigid like a clam. At midnight we got out the Vaseline. Presto. So desired, and yet such an . . . anti-climax. 'Even now I remember dozing against him afterwards, listening to 'Love the One You're With'; wondering how so little could be imbued with so much.'

Mala's grinning: 'And you're still wondering, aren't you?'

Later, Maddie asks: 'Didn't you worry how you'd look without clothes?'

'We kept the lights off.'

'What about the sex itself?'

'Maddie, unlike you, I had regular sex for ten years. I've done it far more than single men in short-term relationships.' I dip a stick of celery into her home-made tahini: 'It's a bit like riding a bike.' She looks at me and we grin. I bite off the tip: 'Bad analogy.'

The barman tops two small glasses of tequila with champagne. He says: 'I'm leaving tonight, girls. These are on the house.' Thumbs over the tops, he bashes them on the bar so they fizz and says: 'Down in one: Very therapeutic.' Tequila slammers. We're slammed already.

'So are you keen on this Nicholas? Nick.'

'He's helping me rediscover myself.'

'Through sex?'

'My body and my soul *are* connected.'

'What's he done for your body?'

'Given it back to me. It used to be Buster's, to do with as *he* wished. Now it's mine again: to do as I wish.'

'And your soul?'

I tip back on the stool, searching for the words. 'I mislaid it – somewhere between the steriliser and the nappy bin. I found it again in a pile of solicitor's letters and an Alannis Morrisette CD.' She laughs. My head's swimming. I say: 'Mala, I've got enough emotional baggage to fill Heathrow, and stretchmarks like a contour map of Snowdon. Despite all that, Nick wanted me. He's boosted my self-esteem – that's the main plank of my rehabilitation.' She's grinning. I say: 'Mala, you know how I look at Buster and see a different man? When you look at me, do I look different to you? Am I new too?'

She considers this carefully: 'You're much more dynamic now – more energised. Your hair's terrific and you've shaped up.' She raises her glass: 'But no, you're not different. You're just the old Nina, restored.'

Music pumps through ceiling speakers: When the Going Gets Tough, the tough get going. My chest and back are wet from sweat. Anne-Marie watches through wary black eyes as I increase my pace on the treadmill: 'To really get that heart going, you should swing your arms,' she says. 'It's aerobic.'

'I only want to tone up.'

'Think about definition; muscle tone. We could get you on to weights – you could look like Her in twelve months time.'

Her is eighteen in a bra top and pedal-pushers. I say:

'Anne-Marie, I'm a mother of two with enough spare rolls to feed the five thousand.'

She makes a note on my 'one-to-one' fitness sheet. 'What's your goal weight?'

'I don't have a goal weight.'

She enunciates slowly as if I haven't understood: 'How much would you like to lose over the next few weeks?'

'Nothing! I just want to get fit – kick a ball with my kids.'

She sighs and checks my heart rate: 'Did you see our thought for the day on the blackboard outside?'

'I didn't notice.'

'It says: self-delusion is pulling in your stomach when you step on the scales.'

In the car I'm playing Steps: 'One For Sorrow'.

Jack says: 'That's what Daddy did to you, isn't it Mummy? He broke your heart?'

'Yes, Darling, he did.'

'But you didn't break his, because he's got Christine.'

Lilla is screaming; out of control. Tears are rolling down her face. She shouts at me about her father: 'He promised he'd always be with me!'

I call Buster at his chambers. I say: 'Buster, could you pop in on your way home and just have a little word with her?'

I have jammed a chair against the study door to stop Lilla bursting in behind me. She is braying, half-demented. I am ready to rip my own head off. If only to save hers.

Buster says: 'I can't Nina, I've promised to give Tony a lift to the station.'

'This is a crisis! Can't he take a cab?'

'I've promised now. Put her on the phone if you like.'

'Buster, you can hear the child. She needs to *see* you.'

'I'm sorry, Nina; can't do.'

It will be the one and only time I call Buster on behalf of his children. The lesson is learned. Buster has life choices. We don't. I don't.

In a single act, my husband and an unknown woman determined my life's path without consultation, consideration or compassion.

Think about that – because it happens every day. That is what husbands, even good husbands, do to their wives with little or no hesitation.

Confession is an act of violence against the innocent. I am a battered wife. No: a *battened* wife.

The children are in bed. I put on Pulp: When did you first realise, it's time you took another lover, baby. The doorbell goes.

'Surprise surprise!': Mala, her friend Caroline Chong, and an Indian takeaway. They march into the kitchen in a nicotine fug from Caroline's Marlboro. Mala winks as they unpack the curries: 'I thought you might need dating tips from a pro.'

Caroline drawls: 'The most important lesson of dating, Nina, is never be the first to call.'

The chicken chat is nicely soured. She pushes it away, her face screwed up distastefully. I say: 'I'm not looking for anything serious. Just some lighthearted fun.'

'Define fun.'

'I've two dysfunctional children and a divorce pending. I only have time for flirting.'

'In other words, she doesn't want Mr Right, but Mr Wrong.' Mala scratches her head: 'I thought we asked for Peshwari nans?'

'We did. Two Peshwari and an onion kulcha. Even Mr Wrong needs to be reeled in slowly, Nina. You mustn't be over keen.'

'I've got microwave rice if you want it, Mala.' I turn back to Caroline: 'Surely older men are past game playing?'

'Of course not. They've got rarity value.'

'Like rhino horn?' Mala picks up the phone: 'I'm calling the Koh-i-Noor to complain.'

I say: 'I'm only looking for company and conversation.'

Caroline says: 'You mean someone who'll help you forget Buster?'

How can I forget Buster when there are two permanent reminders?

Four weeks after Buster left, Lilla asked: 'Is Daddy a bad man?'

I said: 'No, Sweetheart.'

'But he's married to you and living with another lady!'

I said: 'Your daddy's not a bad man, Lilla, but he's been stupid. Grown-ups do stupid things sometimes.'

'Will he go to hell?'

'He's still young. He can make up for his mistakes.'

We talk for two hours. She asked questions I didn't think entered a seven-year-old's head: Did Christine know Daddy had children/If so, why didn't she stop him leaving? Lilla said: 'Is Daddy like Prince Charles? Does he not love you any more, Mummy?'

'He thinks he doesn't, but I think he does.'

'Did he tell you he doesn't love you, Mummy?' I turned away. She asked again: 'Did he tell you he doesn't love you, Mummy?'

'Well, he did, but I don't believe him.'

She took my hand: 'Oh Mummy, I'm so sorry.' She kissed it. 'I'm so sorry.' I said good night and went to my room. She followed me, silently. I turned and saw tears pouring down her cheeks. I put my arms out to her and she clasped me so tightly I caught my breath. And then she started to sob.

* * *

The next day Jack told Buster: 'Daddy, you're a stupid man.'

'Why am I stupid?'

'Because you went away. Mummy says you're stupid to do that.'

Buster shouted: 'How dare you, Nina? You're turning my children against me!'

How can I forget Buster when I am now spending every other weekend in Maddie's spare bedroom so he can come back into our home for two days with Lilla and Jack?

How can I forget Buster with his inept good-night calls on alternate evenings; his silly shilly-shallying over the minutiae of life; the eight o'clock cut-off on occasional week-night visits: 'I'm sorry children but I've a long drive home.'

And then there was the argument over who owned the Dyson.

I was walking in after my weekend away. He was walking out after his weekend in. I didn't want to talk. When a man can't articulate why he left you, and that's the only thing you want to know, conversations become circular and pointless.

Buster said: 'Christine and I haven't got a Hoover. You've got two. I'm going to take the new one.'

'You can't do that!'

'Why not?'

'Because it belongs here. Anyway, the other one's broken. If Christine needs a cleaner, tell her to ask for *her* old one.'

'I own that Dyson, Nina.'

'We both own it Buster: and you can't have it.'

He pulled it one way, I pulled it the other. Minutes later he stormed down the path, shouting. 'You'll be hearing from my solicitor about this!'

*   *   *

How can I forget Buster when *he* won't let me? When he comes to the door and takes the children in his arms as he did every day for seven years? When he puts his feet on the kitchen table in that old familiar way and expounds his theories on law, life, the universe and everything. When he drags behind me like a little puppy: 'Why can't we be friends, Nina?'

How can I forget Buster when he doesn't want me to?

But not forgetting is not the same as remembering.

Spring is slipping into summer. The blossom is out and I am reinventing myself. I no longer worry about what might have been. As Buster manufactured reasons for leaving me, so I refashion my reasons for staying with him: for loving, marrying and supporting him. The truth is, I no longer remember why. I just did, that's all.

'How often do you see Nick?'

'Every eight to ten days.'

'Is there more to him than sex?'

'Sex is enough at this stage.'

Maddie sighs and rolls out the dough, checking its depth with a small measuring stick. 'How did life degenerate so? Five months ago you were happily married.'

'Correction Maddie: I thought I was happily married. The fact that my husband buggered off, suggests I wasn't.'

'Who's to say? You always *appeared* happy.' She rerolls the dough, covering it with Cling Film before putting it into the fridge. 'I find it all so confusing. It makes me question everything and trust nothing. I hate being unsettled. Watching you both, it's like you're on self-destruct. Now you're filing for divorce. At this rate, you'll have nothing left to save.'

Three weeks after Buster left, he and Christine got a flat together.

I said 'Buster, what is it about Christine that you love?'

I expected to hear that she was beautiful, funny, clever.

He replied: 'She gives me space, she never criticises, she listens to what I say and she's interested in what I do.'

I nodded. Of course. His leaving was nothing to do with me, or even with her. It was all about him. She allowed him to be himself: Buster the hero, Buster the lover, Buster the king. Not like me: Buster the husband, Buster the father, Buster the provider of all things.

Because she gave him 'space', he loved her sickliness, her immorality, her dull hair, her fear of spiders. Things he hated in others. And of course, she didn't have two children with whom he had to jostle for attention.

When a man so determinedly puts his immediate needs before those of his family, he is utterly lost. There *is* nothing to save.

Whitsun. Jack keeps his finger on the bell until Maddie answers. The twins call out and four small pairs of feet stampede up the stairs to admire the new Batman duvet covers. Susannah, the nanny, runs up behind them as Maddie gets her jacket and comes out into the sunshine where our cab is waiting.

'I feel I never see you.'

'In the old days you moaned you saw me too much.'

'Because you were always poking fun at the way I do things.'

'Sister's prerogative.' I smile at this woman who is both the bain and the mainstay of my life: 'I do come and squat in your spare bedroom every other weekend, Mads, but it's my only freedom as a single woman. I can't sit in making orange custard and caramelised pears.'

She sighs as we get out at the Tate: 'You still have responsibilities.' Mounting the gallery steps she asks: 'What do we want first, food or Freud?' And then, as we head for the restaurant: 'I suppose you'll be out on the razzle again this Friday? You can't do the same things as single women, because you're *not* a single woman, Nina.' She looks pained: 'You're something in-between.'

'What do in-between people do: stay at home and study prayerbooks? Sew clothes for African orphans? Cook?'

Maddie sighs: 'I'm just saying that . . . perhaps it's time you acted your age.'

What's the Mae West line about marriage as an institution?

When we come out of our marriages we are institutionalised. We stagger into the sunshine, blinking after years of being locked into routines and lifestyles we long ago stopped questioning. Mostly we stop questioning because they work in our favour. We like them. Other times, we stop questioning because the answers are too painful to face. Whatever.

I say to Maddie: 'The trouble is, Sis, my only experience of being single pre-dates my having children. I can't act my age because I don't know how to be my age in this situation.'

Laura calls. 'Stop acting the outlaw, Nina. My kids are desperate to see Lilla and Jack.'

'It's my weekend off. Buster's due any minute.'

'Then bring them next week. I've got loads to tell you.' A pause. 'I'm missing you. If you can't bear the couples thing, I'll make sure Alan's out so it's just the two of us. Okay?'

'Okay.'

My single friend Liz is thirty-six. When the rest of us were succumbing to first love, she was away backpacking. She was always on the move. Now, she's getting broody, but she can't find a man. She says: 'You're so lucky to have Lilla and Jack.'

I look at her blankly. 'Why?'

She throws back her head and laughs: 'Oh Nina, you're so funny.'

I say: 'It only works with two of you, Liz. Look at me now, I'm running to stand still.'

A voice in my ear. 'Do you want to dance?'

'Why not?'

We put down our drinks and squeeze on to the small dance floor. Marvin Gaye: 'Sexual Healing'. He holds me tight, like he's scared I'll slip out of his grasp. 'Will you come back with me?' I'm drunk. I giggle. At the bar, Liz is chatting with his friend. His mouth grazes my ear. 'Come back and cuddle.'

'I'm not going to sleep with you.'

'Then have a cup of tea. I'm only round the corner.'

We're back in the small West Hampstead club where I took Buster that first night we met. At two a.m. I find myself walking back with him. Danny. Looks like Robson Green; younger; a musician. He really does make tea. And two mind-blowing vodkas.

We sit on the bed in his minimalist bedroom. He's reading *Memoirs of a Geisha*. He kisses me. That's it. Sex play. No penetration. An artificial righteousness barrier. He says: 'Stay with me tonight.' So I do.

We wake at ten and he starts again. I panic. I use his phone to call Maddie and tell her I'm okay. My tongue is swollen from dehydration. Like a giant caterpillar in my mouth.

When I return at midday, my sister says nothing. I slope upstairs to the spare room. Then I hear her shouting behind me: 'Are men all you can think about, Nina?'

'Mummy, why won't you play with me?'

'I will, Lilla. Just give me five minutes of quiet first.'

'You don't want quiet! You just want to go on the phone. You talk to everybody but *me*.'

'Oh Sweetheart, that's not true.'

'You don't care what *I* do any more.'

I look at my daughter and know she is right. That in recent months I've been parenting on auto-pilot. 'What is it you want me to do, Lilla?'

'Sit with me. Talk. Play with me and Jack like you used to.'

'How did I play with you?' I throw my hands in the air despairingly. 'Tell me. *Please*. I've forgotten.'

She gives me a look of pure hatred and leaves the room.

'What's gone wrong with me, Mala? I've lost the plot.'

'You're rewriting it.'

'But my priorities are upside down.'

'Your priorities have changed.'

'What about the children?'

'They see your dilemma. You're working things through. They just don't like it. You've got every day of the next twenty years to put those relationships right.'

'I'm obsessed with men.'

'You're rebuilding your self-esteem. It'll pass.'

'So all this behaviour is normal?'

'That's certainly how I remember it.'

'But you don't bother with men now?'

'I told you – it passes.'

I pace around Laura's kitchen as our kids go wild together. I don't want to talk about the Keslake Park Residents' Association or the school fair. She watches me across the room: sympathetic, curious. I turn on her: 'You're judging me, aren't you?'

'I don't think so. Your whole life's gone pear shaped. I'm interested in how you're dealing with it.' She pulls a cake out of the oven. Madeira. 'I think you're doing brilliantly. We all do.' She senses my resentment. 'I meant that kindly.'

'I can't play happy families, Laura. I haven't got one.'

I move to the kitchen door and watch the children in the Wendy house. 'When I was with Buster, this was all so natural to me. Now I'm a misfit.'

She smiles: 'Is that why you're wearing a Wonderbra to do the school run?'

They're playing oldies on Liberty.

Suddenly, on impulse I run into the garden and spin in the rain.

I open my mouth and swallow. Acid rain. Purple rain.

I sing along with the radio: Gloria Gaynor, 'I Will Survive'.

My neighbour calls out from her upstairs window: 'Are you going mad, Nina?'

I laugh aloud: 'No. I'm just being wild and free.'

She shakes her head: 'Don't publicise it. Half the men in north-west London are already getting a hard time because of you.'

'Do we have to watch *Return of the Killer Slugs*, Nicholas?'

'You're the one who wanted to get a video.'

'Not this.'

'I love horror films.'

'I don't.'

'Think of it as part of your learning curve, Nina. You've entered Bloke Country now. Blokes watch horror films.'

I roll over on the bed and try to look seductive. He kisses me. He is just the best kisser. As always this minor fusion leads to mad groping. Until, that is, the slugs start coming up through a sink in the main character's house. With his hand down the back of my jeans, Nick rolls on to his stomach to watch the rest of the film.

It's just like being married.

Laura says: 'After what happened with Buster, why the hurry to find a new man?'

'I miss their input; their humour; their energy. They're not all the same, are they?'

'When things like this happen, I start to wonder.'

'You and Alan are all right.'

'Not always. Not in the way you and Buster were. You can't take anything for granted.'

'That doesn't stop one hoping. Maybe I'll be second-time lucky.'

She smiles: 'And do you know what you're looking for?'

'It's early days yet.'

But I know what I'm *not* looking for. Buster.

I find Mala by Holborn tube, eating a McDonald's. She's with her solicitor friend from Leicester. 'You're late: Jan and I got hungry.'

'You've got ketchup on your blouse.'

'That's all right. I'm only here as an impartial observer.'

Jan, down in London for an Old Bailey case, grins: 'Impartial rather than uninterested?'

They grin at each other. 'Come on, Nina. Into the gates of hell.'

The Villa Stefano is heaving with office crowds. Near the bar is a hen-night table piled high with drinks; the bride-to-be in a white veil pinned with condoms and L plates. We laugh cynically.

At the bar, besuited men in their forties move in on groups of twenty somethings. Jan whispers: 'The last time we were here, a Big Swinging Dick from the Law Society was snogging a girl half his age on the dance floor.'

Mala gets a round. 'I'm putting tonight on exes: you're

CNN's London bureau chief, Nina, and Jan is Middle-East correspondent.'
'Is this where you'd normally bring them?'
She grins: 'You've got a point. All right, let's turn you into a Commander from the Metropolitan Police and an out-of-town solicitor – then it's only half a lie.'
'You know my boy's thinking of joining the police, Mala?'
'Dean? He's only sixteen.'
'He's got the forms.'
'And a big truncheon?' I ask innocently.

Buster says: 'Why can't we be friends, Nina?'
'How can we be friends after what you've done to us?'
'We're going to be in constant contact for years.'
'Then we'll be friendly. That's the best I can manage.'

A man at the bar starts chatting. He admits to being married: unhappily, he claims. Handsome but overweight, he says: 'You should have seen me ten years ago, I was so good-looking the women fell at my feet.'
I say: 'Same here. I was a cracker.'
He motions to our respective girths: 'If this is what marriage does to you, why do we bother?'
He's animated and amusing; we dance. 'After The Love Has Gone': Earth Wind and Fire. We talk about his wife and children: three under the age of seven. 'That's why you're miserable,' I say. 'You're both stressed and you're taking it out on each other. That isn't a bad marriage. It's what happens when you have a family.'
'How long will it take for the stress to pass?'
'About another ten years.'
'I could be dead in another ten years.'
'Only if you're lucky.'

*   *   *

'Darling, you look so tired.'

'I'm all right, Mum.'

'Perhaps you shouldn't go out so much.'

'I'm sorry. I haven't stopped to think about *you*, once, have I?'

'I didn't mean that. I'm happy to babysit every night if that's what you want. I'm just wondering if constant socialising is the best way to get over a marriage.'

'I'm in the house all day. I need an escape.' She says nothing. 'I get lonely, Mum. When I'm out, I feel free.'

'But you're not free. Perhaps it's time to slow down.'

My dancing partner says: 'How come you and your husband didn't sit tight through the ten years of stress?'

I shrug: 'I don't think he realised it was mutual.'

'So I should be grateful that my old lady's still there?'

'You should talk. Acknowledge the problems.'

'Then I'd have to stay.'

'Isn't that why you married?'

In the weeks after Buster went, I spent hour after hour reeling back through our relationship, looking for editing faults. I couldn't find them. I said to him: 'Buster, why did you go?'

'You *know* why I went.'

'Because you fell in love with Christine?'

'Not just that. Things weren't right.'

'What wasn't right?' He'd shake his head and turn away. 'What wasn't right, Buster? We did happy things, didn't we? We didn't bore each other. We made love up to the last moment, we played with the children, we ate, drank, had holidays. Tell me something tangible.'

'I did tell you, Nina. You didn't notice.'

'How could I *not* notice? You and the kids were my life! I noticed everything. I knew you were unhappy at the end, but when I asked, you grumbled about money. I thought that was it.'

'And you were wrong.'

When did the rot set in? Why didn't I smell it? Where were the marker flags that herald disaster? I say: 'Buster, three months before you started seeing Christine, we went to Rome for a romantic break. Your idea. How can things unravel so quickly?'

He shrugs: 'It's happened now. Shall I see the children on Wednesday?'

At two a.m. Mala calls it a day. 'My hair stinks of fags, Nina. I've had enough. Vamoose.'

We walk down to Soho for coffees at Bar Italia. It's mid-June. Chilly. Jan says: 'I haven't been up this late in ages.'

'By choice, you mean.'

She laughs: 'Yes, by choice.'

I say: 'Since Buster went, the kids have nightmares and creep into my bed. I woke up one night with Lilla half on top of me like a giant radiator and Jack lying sideways with his feet resting on my neck.'

Mala scoops the chocolatey froth from her cappuccino and slurps it off the spoon: 'It's the nearest you'll get to a decent man.'

'It's certainly the nearest I *should* get to a decent man.'

Jan says: 'Why does conversation always come back to men?'

Mala perks up: 'It's true, isn't it? Men talk about work or cars or sport, and women always talk about men.' She pulls out a notebook and scribbles a few words: 'I feel a feature coming on.'

'I can't see you next week, Nina. It's England versus Rumania on Monday; Tuesday it's Scotland against Morocco. On the

Wednesday and Thursday we've got corporate entertainments; on Friday its England v. Colombia and Saturday I've a stag night. I'll call on Sunday.'

'Mummy, what's the date?'
  'It's June 26th.'
  'I mean, is it Friday?'
  'Yes, Jack.'
  'Is Daddy going to come?'
  'Yes, it's Daddy's weekend. I'll be at Maddie's.'
  'I miss you when you're gone, Mama.'
  'And I miss you Little Feller. But it's good for you to see Dad.'
  'Why can't I see you both?'
  'Because it doesn't work that way any more.'

'Nick, I think we should call it a day.'
  'Why?'
  'Because this isn't one thing or another.'
  'I thought you didn't want commitment?'
  'Would seeing more of each other mean commitment?'
He shrugs. I say: 'I feel like I'm just filling a gap.'
  'You *told* me you didn't want ties.'
  'I think there's a middle ground between attachment and *de*tachment, which is what I feel from you.' He gets up and turns on Radio Two, as if in doing so, I'm automatically switched off. A song from long ago. Foreigner: 'I Want To Know What Love Is'. I put my arms around him and hold him to me. He's stiff; awkward. Offended. I say: 'I don't understand why you're put-out. If it's not sport, it's work. You've no room in your life for a woman.'
  He shakes me off like a bad smell. 'I don't suppose you'll be wanting to go out tonight.'

Gavin smiles across the table: 'I'm really pleased you came.'

'A last-minute change of plan.'

'A penny for them. I guess it's over with young Nick?'

I smile: 'You're right, but I was actually wondering if Buster bathed the kids before bed.'

He puts his hand over mine: 'You know Maddie and I are always here for you. You only have to say.'

I smile across at this dear man we all take for granted and wonder how I never before noticed his kindess, his patience, his smile. Somehow, all other men diminished in Buster's company; he dominated the skyline; absorbed all attention. Now I sit with friends and marvel at their partners. I marvel at Gavin who has loved my sister unquestioningly since university days.

Maddie says: 'Are you sure you want beef, Nina? I don't trust it, whatever the source.'

'I'll risk the BSE, thanks.'

We're in Mezzo, entertaining Dome folk: out-of-town engineers – two married, one female. And one designer, Tag, too pretty, very attentive. He leans into me: 'I don't normally like mad cows, but I don't see any froth around your mouth.'

Within two weeks Tag and I have a night out together. Afterwards, we spend hours sitting on his sofa, kissing and talking. Nothing else. He puts on a CD. Jennifer Paige: *Crush*. He says: 'I don't know what I feel about you Nina, but I do know that even after this little time, I'd do anything you ask.'

'Not *anything*.'

'I don't deny the attraction.' He kisses my face. 'Right now, this is the only way in which I can express the closeness I feel for you; but we're at different stages of our lives.' He rests his head on mine. 'This is too important to be a fling, and it can't be anything else.' A pause. 'You're an older woman with children.'

I say: 'I'm not suggesting happy ever after, Tag. I'm still married to Buster for goodness' sake. But why can't we fool around and dissipate this awful tension?'

'Because this is more than that.'

'But it *can't* be more. You said yourself we're at different stages in our lives. It *must* end.'

'No. We'll be friends for ever.'

I laugh: 'Why is there so much self-destruction in this game?'

Liz says: 'Do you sometimes wish you'd married Mark Landsman instead of Buster?'

'I don't think so.' We hang on to the sides, treading water as the other early-morning swimmers crossly tut at us blocking the deep end. 'Mark and I were so caught up in each other it felt base. It was selfish; unnatural.'

'Isn't that what Buster finds so moreish about Christine?' I shrug. 'Why did you feel *he* was the better bet?'

I wash out my goggles while I think about it. 'Buster didn't make my heart race, but I was turned on by his cleverness, his calm, his confidence. Mark was sex on legs, which clouded his other qualities: warmth, wit, wisdom.'

I think about Tag. I was like him. Always planning ahead; weighing up the pros and cons. Looking for the best bet. Unwilling to take risks with *the rest of my life*. Under the water Liz grabs me by the legs and I'm submerged. We race back down to the shallow end. She pulls off her hat, thick red hair falling damply to her shoulders. 'Maybe I should have learned from you. I always thought good sex was as important as conversation. It clouded my judgement.'

'There's still time.'

'Maybe.' She starts to climb out. 'You don't regret Mark?'

'No. Mark's my perennial "what if" – but he's my past. Buster was my future. Does that make sense?'

*　　*　　*

Tag starts calling every evening.

When I put down the phone he says 'Good night Darling.'

Lilla is trying to get through to the Disney Channel and win tickets to *Mulan*. 'I know the answer, Mummy – it's China.'

Jack is 'fixing' his trike on the kitchen table: 'Is Daddy coming today?'

'No Darling, tomorrow.'

'Will he put us to bed?'

'If he isn't in a hurry.' I stop and check myself. 'I'm sure he'll *want* to put you to bed Darlings, but sometimes it's difficult.'

My mother comes into the kitchen: 'Nina, why don't you go out now while they're both happy. The longer you leave it, the more they'll fret.'

'Are you having collagen injections?'

'No – it's a special cream you put on before your lip pencil. Great isn't it?'

Liz scrutinises my face carefully. 'You're all sparkly.'

'Face glitter.'

'How much are all these cosmetics costing?'

'Does it matter?'

Men and make-up: the first steps to recovery.

My cosmetics bag now travels separately on the passenger seat of my car. Instant gratification at every second traffic light.

Soon I'll have to consider the third step to recovery: work. But not before the day-to-day problems are out of the way.

I sit with my solicitor, admiring, through his window, the

huge hanging baskets that proliferate from the lamp-posts in Westminster. He says: 'Too many begonias. They ought to be more original.' In the corner a large rubber plant is obscuring the filing cabinets. He pours the dregs of his drink into its pot and checks the divorce deposition. 'This is fine. If we send it off in the morning, the Decree Nisi will be through in about seven weeks. We've just made the deadline before quickie divorces bite the dust.' He leans back and smiles at me through his beard: 'You're quite sure you want to go through with this, Mrs Goodholme?'

'Why shouldn't I be?'

'A huge number of spouses regret rushing at it.'

'Mr Preston, my husband has set up home with another woman. What is there to regret?'

'He may change his mind at some point. You may decide that, despite what he's done, you want him back.'

I shake my head. I say: 'Mr Preston, I've got the children; I've got the house; I've got the car; and, for the time-being, I've got the maintenance. Soon I'll return to work. All I've lost is the man. In other words, the easiest component to replace.

'You've become so tough, Nina.'

'I'm not tough, Maddie – I've just taken charge. Bloody hell! Thirty-six *pounds* for a giant mushroom?'

'They're a delicacy.'

'Thirty-six *pounds*? How can anyone justify asking that? And it's filthy – look at it.'

'They're rarer than truffles, Nina. All you need is a sliver to provide flavour for a whole dish. Put it down if you don't want it.' Sniffing, she works her way across the Harvey Nichols' food department. 'You've become very cynical.'

'What does that mean?'

'You think the worst of everybody. Your bad luck isn't enough of a reason to be so sour about the rest of us.'

'Is this because I said you should check Gavin isn't getting his sexual kicks elsewhere? I was just joking.'
'It didn't sound like you were joking.'

My mother says: 'You mustn't have a go at Maddie. It isn't her fault Buster's gone.'
'Well of course it isn't.'
'Then don't upset her by suggesting it's her turn next. You're grown-ups now.'

A silly remark about Gavin suddenly resonates with accusation. Every aside from the lips of the afflicted is imbued with hidden meaning. My presence evokes a fear of magical contagion: I'm a curse at the dining tables of the chattering classes. Here is Nina alone with her children: manless; meaningless; dismembered.
Kevin Preston says: 'Is the man really the easiest component to replace?'

My old boss, Samir, invites me for lunch: 'I heard the news. I thought maybe it was time you started planning for the future.'
'Meaning?'
'Meaning that you start subscribing to *Campaign* and *Media Week* and think about what you've got to offer.'
He tells me his theory on love. 'The way I see it, Nina, is this. Everyone has a number of perfect partners. Each will be different in his or her own way; but all will be compatible in the long term.' He orders more mineral water. 'I believe we meet a potential life partner every three or four years, but for various reasons – youth, work, other interests – we won't automatically commit ourselves.' I nod into my herb bread. 'Once we get to our late twenties and early thirties, the urge to settle comes over most of us. At this stage we'll almost certainly marry the next all-round candidate who presents themselves.'

'And we all live happily ever after, right?'

He purses his lips: 'Yes. Except . . . The problem then, Nina, is that the cycle doesn't end. Even after we marry, we'll periodically meet other men or women who we know we could love; could live with. The hard part then is to walk away, and to cherish what you've already got.'

We order coffees. Samir says: 'Now we've got business out of the way, the point I'm making to you is that another Mr Right *will* come along; and if, for any reason, that doesn't work out, then there'll be another one. The world is full of possibilities.'

'Rose Davis. Ran the "George Davis is innocent" campaign. Got him out and bang – he's videoed at another blagging.' Mala sits pen in hand. 'Remember?'

'Vaguely.'

'And Joyce McKinney, who kidnapped the Mormon missionary. Kurt something. Said she'd ski naked down Everest with a rose in her teeth if he wanted.' She scratches her ear with the pen.

Caroline says: 'What about Vicky Hodge. As I recall, her boyfriend could balance nine beer glasses on his penis.'

'Fame by association.' We giggle.

Mala's conservatory doors are open to let in the afternoon sun. Our children, however, on the threshold of the summer holidays, are deep inside her house watching *Sabrina the Teenage Witch*.

Caroline says: 'If your sister thinks you're a man-hating bitch, Nina, where does she think you hang out at weekends: dyke conventions?'

'She's talking in broader terms.'

'Does she know about the phone sex with Tag?'

'It's not phone sex, Mala!'

'That's what it sounds like to me.' Suddenly she screeches: 'I know: Sheila Buckley! Stonehouse's secretary – ran off to

Aus after the fake suicide. Where's she today?' Scribbling furiously she adds: 'You should be careful, Nina – or Lilla will come across you playing governess and naughty boy.'

Caroline says: 'Governess and naughty boy? Are we talking private tuition or self-correction?'

'What are you wearing tonight, Nina?'
    'My white nightshirt with the button front.'
    'Where does it stop?'
    'Just past my bottom.'
    'Where are you?'
    'In bed. In the dark.'
    'You're not being naughty, are you?'
    'Are you?'
    'Well, I'm lying down.'
    'Where are your hands?'
    'One's on the phone.'
    'You're all mouth and no trousers, Tag.'
    'No trousers. You're right.'
We giggle. He drops his voice: 'I don't want anyone to hear me.'
    I drop mine: 'In case they come in?'
    'In case I'm coming.' More giggles. He whispers: 'How's your consultancy idea coming along.'
    'All right, I think. Have you been busy?'
    'I'm doubling output.'
    'And you still can't keep up with me.'
In the dark, the whispered banalities about our day are erotic beyond measure. I say: 'So what's the new line?'
    'I'm not going to bore you with that.'
    'Well you're not going to *bore* me with anything else, are you?'
    He laughs aloud. 'My drilling equipment's blunt.'
    'And my bloody well's run dry.'

A sigh: 'I'm crazy about you, Nina. Keep talking to me. I love your voice; I love the things you say.'

'I've been talking to you for the past ninety minutes. It's one o'clock in the morning, Tag.'

'All right, Darling. Goodnight. I'll call you tomorrow.'

'This happens every night?' Caroline shakes her head and pulls on a cigarette.

Mala laughs. 'It's like being a teenager again: making something out of every exchange.' She puts down her pad and stretches. 'Just like I mooned after Josh.'

Caroline says: 'Well he's finally taken the bait, although I'm still not sure it's a good thing.'

'Josh is your brother, Caroline. Don't be mean. Anyway, we really are just friends. You can stop fretting.' Mala yawns and stretches noisily: 'Sister Wendy doesn't count as infamous, does she? It's a shame we can't print pictures of Mary Bell.'

There's a sudden influx of small people.

'Mama.' Jack, so babyish, so sweet, climbs on to my lap. I nuzzle his head and enjoy the wholeness of him.

'I must talk to you about reducing the money, Nina.'

'I'm not earning enough for you to reduce it, Buster.'

'Not immediately. In a few months' time.'

'We've already agreed a formula; why can't we stick to it?'

'Christine and I can't continue in a tiny flat. I need to think about getting a home and having a life.'

'Buster, when marriages break up, one of the partners will come off the worse. Given that I've got the future of two children to consider, I think we should both give thanks that it's you.'

'You're saying I deserve this?'

'No. I'm saying that in the short term, your priority has

to be *us*. Given that you're happily ensconced with your lady love, and I'm still clearing the shit, I don't think it's asking too much that you put your financial ambitions on the backburner.'

'That's typical of you, Nina. You always have to bring it up.'

'Bring what up?'

'The fact that I left you. Don't you think *you* had something to do with it?'

'When did I bring it up? Like what?' In the background Lilla has put on the Tricky CD: *Broken Homes*. I say: 'Buster, let's just get the summer holidays done. Then we can reposition, okay?'

Sometimes, but not so often now, I still burn up inside if my children are giving me a hard time. I look at them and think: why doesn't Buster live through this? What made him think I wanted all this grief?

When men talk about abandonment they always put forward the theory that it takes two to kill a marriage: These things don't happen by chance/The marriage *must* have been in trouble beforehand/Clearly, something about the situation was untenable.

All these options effectively mean the same thing. They also have the same sub-text: no man in his right mind would leave a marriage if the wife wasn't somehow defective in her role.

When women talk about abandonment, their theory is that it takes only one to kill a marriage: I neglected him/I spent too much time on the children/I didn't notice he was so depressed about money or work.

All these options effectively mean the same thing. They also have the same sub-text: the poor man left the marriage because his wife was somehow defective in her role.

It isn't true.

*   *   *

Maddie fine-chops fillet lamb and red onions: 'I'm not saying I don't like the tougher you, Nina. I do. But sometimes you're too harsh; too judgemental.'

'Maddie: I'm just the way I used to be.'

'I lost myself, you know, Maddie.'

'I know.'

'I was so busy rushing around making sure everyone else's life went like clockwork . . . He liked that; so did the kids. I was Mrs Buster Goodholme. When freelance work came in, I was distracted. They'd complain. He said we didn't need the money – but *I* needed some outside interest.'

'You've told me this before.' She turns down the radio. Boyzone: 'Did You Fly Away'.

'Sometimes I wonder if you're sympathetic to Buster going. You're always implying I didn't do my job properly.'

'It's not about right and wrong, is it?'

'What's it about then?'

'It's about all of life's imponderables. Chance; circumstance; opportunity.'

'But we loved each other.'

'Love's a state of mind, Nina, not a form of protection.'

Surely love is both?

When I was expecting Jack, Lilla became very anxious about her place in my heart. I bought and planted some cress seeds. I said to her: 'We're planting love. When the shoots appear, we'll eat them, and the love will stay in our tummies until the baby comes and then we'll give that love to him or her.'

We ate only a few strands. The basic principle had been understood. The capacity for love is within us all; it can be grown and given in infinite quantities without harming those who already benefit from it. Love *does* protect.

Unless it's sexual love; which only works in twos.

Buster comes to collect the last of his books. I corner him in the study. I say: 'Buster, are you still filled with passion?' He looks confused. 'You never mention Christine these days. Has the ardour cooled?'

'Just leave it, Nina.'

'Why didn't you tell me you were unhappy?'

A sigh. 'What's the point of going over this?'

'It bugs me. I need to know where I failed.'

'Isn't it enough that you did?'

I shake my head. The children come running in and he scoops them up, each in turn. I look across at him: so comfortable, so welcoming. So at home. But this is not his home.

I say: 'You know what, Buster? I didn't fail you. You failed yourself.'

I drive home one of Lilla's friends, Clover. They've spent the day arguing over Barbies in the kitchen and fighting over who sits where to watch the Disney Channel, but now it's time to go, everybody's moaning. I pile the kids into the car. Clover says: 'I don't want to go. I want to stay and play.'

'I promised your mummy I'd return you before seven.'

'You don't have to do it just because *she* says so.'

I check their seatbelts and put the car into gear. I say: 'Listen, Clover. Your mum has a bloody hard life. She cares for you and Gino; she goes to college; she sells from catalogues so you never go without. She's there come rain or shine. She's a fantastic woman. Do you know what that tells me about *you*?'

'No.'

'It tells me that you're going to grow up to be a fantastic woman, too. Because you're like her. So don't moan about rules – they're there to help, not hurt you.'

The kids all laugh at this and I'm filled with anger and sadness for all those lone women who raise children with little money and no help. All those women on whom I stood in judgement until I joined their ranks. I look across at Clover, so small and determined. Unlike my children, she doesn't have a rich daddy to soften the blow. She doesn't have grannies all rushing to do their bit. She, like her mother, is bearing the load alone.

Suddenly I want to hug her, to tell her how wonderful she is. And to hug her mother and all those other strong women who soldier on while dodging the brickbats of the righteous. But instead, I say: 'Would you like to come again next week?'

I'm on the floor doing the abdominiser. A shadow falls across my face. Anne-Marie.

'How's it going Nina? You look a bit thinner.'

'I weigh exactly the same.'

'Muscle weighs more than fat – you probably *have* lost weight.' I grit my teeth and do a bit of forward rolling. 'You've tightened up the fat pad under your boobs. We're going to have to work on that tummy though.'

A glorious man in a grey sweatshirt sits on the rower. We both turn to admire his momentous coffee-brown shoulders. A centrifugal force pulls Anne-Marie in his direction. I lie on the floor recovering my breath before the next lot of curls. On the ski machines, two local mothers are discussing antibiotics.

'They say it ruins their immune systems.'

'I'm sure that's true. If we hadn't been prescribed erithromycin for Milly's ear infections, she'd never have needed grommets.'

'Isn't erithromycin a penicillin substitute?'

'Yes, but it's still an antibiotic. Milly vomits with penicillin.'

'George is the same with Benylin. He icks it up at night.'

'What you need is a fleeced mattress protector from John Lewis. It's worth it when you think how much beds cost.'

'I know. Hetty had one made for Max. By Simon Horn. It was over a thousand pounds. It's like something from a story book.'

Slowly I clamber up from the floor. One of the women shouts: 'Nina! How are you? I haven't seen you since Buster went. Oh. I'm sorry. Didn't mean to shout. Are you all right.'

'Yes, Claire, I'm fine.'

'What about the children? They must be a handful now the holidays have started?'

'They're all right. It's a struggle, but we're getting there.'

'You're looking very well.'

'I'm actually exhausted, but thank you.'

'It's time you got yourself a *decent* man. One that appreciates you. You really deserve it after what you've been through.'

'Actually, I've got a decent man, Claire. That's why I'm so tired. He shagged my brains out last night.'

'Naughty girl.'

'She made me angry.'

'I didn't shag your brains out last night.'

'You don't shag my brains out any night, Tag.'

'That's because I'm too busy picking them.'

'They don't fall out of your ears in the middle of the sex act, you know. It's not dangerous.'

'Feeling frustrated, Nina?'

'Why do you do this to me?'

'What do you want me to do to you?'

'I've told you so many times.'

'Tell me again.'

'I want you to kiss me and hold me and – hell, you don't even have to make love to me, Tag. Just let our skin touch.'

Samir takes me to a matinée. He brings an invitation to the BCAF Summer Party. I say: 'Is this the social equivalent of a sympathy fuck?'

'The words you're looking for Nina are "thank you".'

We buy ice-creams and go out on to the parapet of the National Theatre: it's the interval of Tom Stoppard's latest play.

'Thanks for all your advice, Sam. You're right. It's time I got back to work. For personal reasons as well as practical.'

'That's all right. I remember Roni struggling with her options when our youngest reached school age. Look at her now: New York this week, Manilla the next.'

We stop and watch lovers walking beneath us along the riverfront. Two, dreadlocked, stop to kiss. He runs his fingers across her face; she squeezes his bottom in her right hand. Red red fingernails catching the light.

I say: 'I think I'll sort it out when I get back from holiday with the children. Recharging batteries and all that.'

He smiles: 'Then stay away from Spanish waiters.'

We stop as the tannoy announcement comes through. 'Ladies and Gentlemen please take your seats in the Lyttleton Theatre. This afternoon's performance of *The Invention of Love* will resume in three minutes.'

'Mummy, when do we go to Spain?'

'August tenth, Sweetie. Eleven days' time.'

'Will there be a pool?'

'No, but there's a beach near the apartment.'

'So we can make sand castles?'

My heart sinks. 'I suppose so, Lilla,' I say unhappily.

Caroline and I see *The Big Lebowski*. She hates it. We go in search of food. 'Shouldn't you be on a diet, Nina?'
'What for?'
'To concentrate your mind.'
'To concentrate it on what?'
'I don't know. Love, perhaps?'
Crossly, I say: 'Buster didn't run off with a supermodel, Caroline. The one time we met, he described her as "hardly a dolly bird".' We turn into Gerrard Street. 'Anyway, I thought size didn't matter. Aren't forty-seven per cent of all women supposed to be a size sixteen or over?'
'Not the forty-seven per cent who're looking for men.'

'Buster, what have you become?' He's confused. 'You were always so generous and kind. To make a fuss about a milk bill!'
'What fuss? I paid it when I was here last weekend.'
'If you wanted the money back, you should have asked. To deduct it from the children's maintenance cheque is so—'
'What's the big problem, Nina? I've given you money towards the holiday; I'm being more than generous at every level—'
'But it's so petty: to deduct a few measly quid!'
He shakes his head: 'I just don't understand you.'
'And I don't understand *you*!'
We have both lost ten years. Just like that.

I pull on a V-neck white-ribbed T-shirt which emphasises my possession of a balcony-front bra. My size sixteen black pant-suit still fits: curves emphasised, stomach covered. A new colour wash on my hair has turned it a rosy conker: surprisingly engaging.

'On the hunt, are we?'

'Yes, Mum: for work. I told you about the consultancy idea. If I schmooze the right people, they may put stuff my way.'

'You've stopped mourning.' She takes my face in her hands and kisses me on the forehead: 'You know what they say: the greatest revenge is to be happy.'

I kiss her back: 'Then I've got my revenge. I'll never be happy about what happened, but given that I had no choice, I'm happier now than I've been in years. I thought *I* was in charge at home, but I see now that everything, from food to outings, was arranged around Buster's preferences. Now I'm back in control.'

The band blows into 'New York New York'. Great saxophone. The late evening sun has tinted the canvas golden. Inside the marquee are rows of tables and a set wooden dance floor. Through the openings, the square is a mass of well ordered foliage. Men in grey striped Dolce & Gabbana suits are positioned in neat, noisy groups with young women in strappy evening gowns. I stand on my own, on the threshold between outside and in.

'Hello Nina, you're looking beautiful. I was sorry to hear about your marriage break-up.'

I turn round to greet the tall, greying man with the chiselled Michelangelo face. Paul Avedon. 'Hello Paul. You were right: the emeralds were unlucky.'

He laughs: 'I'd forgotten about them. Would you like a top-up?'

'Please.'

He takes my glass, leaving me to hover uncertainly as Eric Casey hoves into view: 'Nina Sutra! You haven't changed a bit. When are you going to come back and infuse our copy with your legendary prose style?'

I say, cockily: 'Whenever you like, Eric.'

'Are you working?'

'I've been copy-editing for Will Davis at Henriques Dudley, but I'm keen to get back in the scrum.'

He looks serious: 'You know we've bought a direct marketing subsidiary? Bugle Direct. Not very sexy, but mail order is the business of the moment. We're pulling in some very upmarket accounts – clothing mostly. It's not high profile and it's not exciting, but we could seriously do with someone who can knock a few words together to flog the lines.'

'Why don't you call me? Samir has my number.'

'I'll do that.'

I can barely breathe as he wanders off.

A squeaky voice behind me: 'How are you, my darling?'

'Cathy! How are you?'

'Very well.' She waves her fingers under my nose: 'Did you know I'd become Mrs Richard Skeller?' I notice the enormous diamond. Richard Skeller, newest partner: still negotiating his name over the door. 'We tied the knot six weeks ago.'

'Congratulations!' We hug. I say: 'Don't ever take it for granted. Always work at it.'

'Hark at you: we're still in the honeymoon phase, Nina. Don't spoil it with all your dark hinting. I knew Buster was a shit, all the time. Remember when I saw him in the Camden Brasserie with that girl? You should have listened. I tried to tell you.'

'She was his colleague. She had MS! He was comforting her.'

She shakes her head. 'No he wasn't. I didn't give you the details because I had a go at him and he begged me not to. His tongue was down her throat and his hand was up her skirt half the night. She didn't look poorly, I promise you.'

I stare at her, disbelieving. Stunned.

A hand on my shoulder: 'Here's your bellini.'

'Thank you.'

'Is something the matter?'

'I was just telling Nina what a shit her ex was, Paul.'

'All exes are shits, Cathy. That's what defines an ex.'

Cathy says: 'I'm too new to the game to hear all this. Give me a ring, Nina, and we can lunch.' I nod as she heads off.

Paul says: 'Are you all right?' Again I nod. He takes my left hand in his. 'I see the emeralds have gone.'

'I lost two of the stones nine months before Buster left. The ring's still with the jeweller. He's probably sold it on by now.'

'And your wedding ring?'

'I threw it away the day we told the kids.' I smile. 'Very dramatic, but it felt right. It still does.'

'You know, Nina, I had a few dealings with Buster when BCAF appealed against the ASA banning the Carpuccio campaign. I thought he was wonderfully clever, but brash and unfriendly. He was redeemed by marrying you. You are *his* loss, he is not yours.'

I notice, suddenly, that we are still holding hands.

One day during another row over money – what else? – Buster will shout: 'Do you know how many of our friends have called me since our marriage ended? Exactly zero. That's how many.'

I say: 'Buster, let's be straight here. For the first six months of your absence, we only had your mobile number. You're rarely in chambers. *How* could people find you? *You* should have rung them.' He goes to speak, but I hold up my hand to finish: 'Our friends invested their time and affection in us for ten years. You repaid them by going back on everything they believed in. It's not that they don't love you: it's just that there's nothing to say.'

*   *   *

Indeed as the months have rolled by, there's been little they can say to *me*. Gone are the days when Buster and I opened a bottle of wine and gossiped with old friends while our kids happily played together. Now, when invited out, the men overcompensate for the sins of their missing brother. They lavish time on Lilla and Jack, and compliment me. The women watch us sadly; kindly. It's only friends who've experienced divorce, or who remain single, that understand the steady highs followed by a sudden gut-wrenching low. Going to bed at four in the morning, starry eyed from some juvenile encounter. Waking up at four in the morning stomach clenched with anger at a remembered slight from Buster.

I call up Mala, feeling wretched: 'That bloody man's having another bad hair day. Is this how it is for you with your exes?'

She giggles: ''Fraid so. Jay calls and cries on my shoulder every time the wife or baby are giving him trouble, and Cal is still blaming me for his creative block. So, what's Buster saying?'

'In the middle of yet another excuse for not coming round to see the kids, he suddenly announced that I couldn't sustain relationships. He's the one that went, Mala!'

'Ignore him.'

'It's not funny! I was in a good mood until then.'

'You're all he's got, Nina. He can't have a go at Christine because he needs her too badly. You're the convenient outlet – a bit like Sainsbury's. Don't take it personally.' She lowers her voice: 'Listen, I can't chat. I'm up for an assistant editorship so I'm looking seriously keen. Let's talk later.'

The Saturday before Spain I have open house. Will Davis who supplies my proofs says: 'Middle-class men have swallowed the line that women can be anyone or anything they choose. They've swallowed it so well, they expect women to be *everything*: worker, wife, mother, organiser and . . . bosom.'

We're listening to Cornershop: everybody needs a bosom for a pillow. Liz and I lounge on the grass as he continues his exposition. 'From the woman's point of view, it's a no-win situation: you either work your bollocks off trying to be all things to all men, or you struggle and get rejected for failing.'

'So it's all the fault of the feminists?' Liz says sweetly.

'No. It's the fault of men who force women to display *su*periority in order to claim *e*quality.'

'But only middle-class men?'

'Well, us diamond geezers,' he says, slipping into Estuary vernacular, 'we believe women can only do so much. When they fail we don't complain: we cosset them and commiserate because we still want to be their protectors. Therefore, one could argue, we're more understanding of the fact that nobody, male or female, can do everything brilliantly.'

Laura and Alan wander out. She says tartly: 'That doesn't mean you treat women as equals.'

'We've always treated them as equals: think of the East End matriarchs. It's just that we don't pretend they're the same.'

Before the three start arguing, I say: 'Well, it's certainly true that Buster feels I failed him, even though I was juggling everything like a headless chicken. But I'm not sure class makes a difference, Will. Men have always needed us as mothers as well as lovers.'

'Don't be so sour.'

Lilla comes running past with Laura's eldest son: 'There's someone ringing the doorbell.'

Samir and Roni come in with a large cake: 'This is the sort of thing your sister would approve of, Nina. Not too late, are we?'

'No. You're just in time to save us from an argument over whether middle-class men or working-class men are the most chauvinistic. Will says middle-class males now expect women to be superior at everything, and if they're not, they're effectively failures; whereas working-class men expect women to be equal in some areas, but not all.'

'Which areas are those?'

Will walks into the room: 'Hackney, Islington, Barnet and, of course, this here wasteland between Harlesden and Hampstead.'

He pours drinks while I pull the Cling Film off a set of haphazardly prepared salads: 'This is the lunch, chaps. I'm afraid, unlike Maddie, cooking is not my speciality.'

Samir says jokingly: 'No wonder Buster left you.'

The period between abandonment and divorce is officially called separation. It is a period of limbo: a time of nothingness. I am a piece of unclaimed land, waiting for someone to plant the flag and name me. When my Decree Absolute comes I will have wholly reconstructed my new, and indeed, my previous self: Nina Sutra. Until then, I am still legally attached to Buster.

I am stateless. Status-less.

'Would you marry again?

'Absolutely.'

'How will you know you've got it right next time?'

'I didn't get it wrong the first time, Liz. It just *went* wrong.'

Kevin Preston calls as the cab arrives to take me and the children to the airport. 'Your Decree Nisi comes through on Friday.'

'Great!'

'My advice is we hold off applying for the Absolute

until the money's settled. In the unfortunate event of Mr Goodholme dropping dead, this protects your rights as his wife.'

We are on the beach when I realise that I have never swum in the sea. It scares me. I like pools where I can see the bottom. And where people would see me if I sank to the bottom. I do not like dense water which ebbs and flows and fools the eye. Dense water with hundreds of bodies in it so no one person is easily discernible; identifiable. Lilla and Jack are wearing armbands, but I won't let them into the water. They shout and stamp their feet: 'But we always play in the sea!'

We compromise on paddling where the depth is no more than waist height. 'I don't care if you're not frightened kids: I am.' But, bored with my restrictions, they want to make sand castles. I say: 'For goodness' sake let me just lie here and read a book – it's my holiday too!'

They start crying: 'But Daddy always let us swim in the deep bits. Daddy always built castles with us.'

Yes. Daddy took them out far into the sea – in his arms, on his back, in little inflatable dinghys. He splashed with them and ducked them, he let them take risks, knowing he was strong enough and confident enough to prevent any great horrors. He sat on the sand for hours digging with them. They made giant holes with seats in each corner so the four of us could sit inside and tell each other stories. Sometimes they were so comfortable, I'd sit and read until the tide came in and destroyed them. They built sand castles. Buster had the broadest shoulders – he shifted sand like a St Bernard in the snow. He and Lilla would make huge pies fashioned into fantastical fortresses. My job was to build the turrets. I had a speciality – cone-shaped turrets with wet sand dribbled on and down them like something from a cartoon. Ferrets, we called them.

Whole afternoons were spent on swimming, digging and construction.

Now I am alone on the beach with the children and I cannot manage any of it. I'm not interested. I wouldn't be interested even if I were a serious swimmer; even if I were a serious sand artist. Bodies. So many bodies. And all that terrifying water.

The children look at me with grave disappointment. What's the point of being here if Mummy can't make the holiday worthwhile?

By the end of two weeks I am depressed and exhausted and the children are disillusioned and miserable. We all have new books and T-shirts because that's what mummies do on holiday – read and shop. The odd sand castle has been built; the odd water adventure has happened around rock pools where I feel nominally in charge. But all in all, I've failed to make them happy. I've failed to make myself happy. We've been shortchanged.

Is a shortchange as good as a rest?

'Ten days felt like a lifetime. I missed you.'

'A little bit or a big bit?'

'I don't have any little bits.'

'Why should I believe you have any big bits without evidence?'

'Would you like to put my big bit in the witness box?'

'I think that's the only place I'll see it standing up, Tag.' He laughs. I say: 'Mala's right. This is like phone sex. Are we ever going to have a relationship?'

'Why spoil a brilliant friendship?'

'How can it be brilliant when I can barely remember what you look like?'

'How often do you see your other friends?'

'It doesn't matter. What we have in common is shared history. We've done things together, seen things together.

There's been a courtship, just as there is in any set of human relations.'

'All right, we'll go to a movie. Just you and me.'

'I'm going to have a turkey night.'

'It's very hard to get turkey just right, you know, Nina. You'll have to cook it upside down.'

'I'm not *cooking* a turkey. I mean a night like a hen night: a sort of celebration between the Nisi and the Absolute. We'll call it a turkey night because we're older and bulkier.'

'Is a celebration appropriate?'

'Of course, Maddie, get real.' I laugh: 'Wait till the divorce. I'm going to have the biggest party ever.' She sniffs disapprovingly. I say: 'I have no need to feel guilty. For ten years I put marriage first. Now I'm putting myself first.' I hold my hands out for her to inspect: 'They're clean. I'm released to be whoever or whatever I want to be.'

When I was younger, I used to say that the finest way I could imagine dying would be to drive into a wall at 150mph playing Janis Joplin, 'Me and Bobby McGee', at a thousand decibels.

It comes into my mind every now and then when I see Buster looking ragged.

Freedom's just another word for nothing left to lose.

I put down the iron and answer the phone. Eric Casey. 'Nina, how are you?'

'Brilliant, Eric. Yourself?'

'Don't ask. We're going public next year. I didn't realise so much paperwork was involved.'

I balance the phone on my shoulder and put a crease in Lilla's jeans. 'It's incredibly tiring, becoming a multi-millionaire.'

He laughs. 'If I'm correct, when I saw you at the Summer Party you said something about setting up a consultancy?'
'Yes.'
'Well, you'll remember what I said about our direct marketing arm. Amanda Crowley's now decided not to return from maternity leave and Jaspal Singh's been headhunted by Broigus Temper and Hatchet so we're using this as an opportunity for a major overhaul.' He clears his throat: 'I wondered, as you're on the market, if you might enjoy stepping in for a while. We need someone who can feel their way around a few accounts, get a sense of what's working and what's missing. A number of projects need putting on track.'

I put down the iron and lean against the wall. I say something like 'Ummm.' Jack looks up, to ask something. I put my finger to my lips and, miraculously, he goes back to his toys.

Eric says: 'I know it's been some years since you were here, but the key to getting it right is language. You've always been so good with words. I don't think you'll have a problem. Axel Manley's in charge of pictures. The two of you always enjoyed working together.' A pause: 'We'd need you fairly urgently. And, of course, I'll pay the standard consultancy rate.'

My heart is doing backflips. He's effectively asking me to be an account manager, albeit on below the line projects. I say: 'The children are home until September third.'

'Start the following Monday – the seventh. Perhaps take it through to Christmas.'

As he rattles through various details, I'm grinning fit to burst. I put the phone down and grab Jack and Lilla. We turn the stereo up high and dance around the sitting room in sheer delight. Will Smith: 'Gettin' Jiggy With It'.

Laura and I take the children to the zoo. Entry alone

is £23. I sigh into my empty purse: 'Thank God I'll be earning soon.'

'You know I'll have the kids, don't you? They can have tea and play with my boys till you're back from work.'

'Five children, five afternoons a week?'

'I love Lilla and Jack. Don't leave them with a stranger. They'll keep the boys busy. It would give me space.'

'Then I'll pay you.'

'We don't need money.'

'But it'd make *me* feel better.' I stop and hug her to me: 'You don't know what this means, Laura.'

'You've worked miracles in the past few months. We're all on your side – you know that.'

Suddenly I'm crying. 'I so wanted to be a good mother.'

'There are lots of different ways of being a good mother, Nina.'

The Goodholmes take Lilla and Jack for the last few days of the summer break. Even as I shut the door with relief, I feel a pang at their departure.

When I meet Liz at Café Rouge, I'm exhausted. I say: 'It's only now that I appreciate how parents work as a team – distilling information, answering questions, finding new angles. I'm always running behind them, instead of leading.'

'Meaning?'

'There were so many things Buster and I talked about over breakfast or dinner: the day's news, politics, history, ideas, gossip – there was so much for the kids to pick up on. Now there's just me in a state of stress, Lilla with the Bunty, and Jack making plane noises over the chocolate Ready Brek.'

Liz shrugs: 'Your kids are hardly going to point the finger because you didn't explain the detail of Monica Lewinsky's blow jobs to them.'

*   *   *

Tag and I go to see *Saving Private Ryan*. I act frightened
in the gory bits, hoping he'll pull me to him. There's
no movement. Afterwards we walk arm in arm around
the side streets of central London, looking for somewhere
to eat, ending up at Veeraswamy's, a grand old Indian
restaurant revamped in modern bistro style. Our table
overlooks a little cut-through filled with South American
restaurants and up-market strip joints. Swallow Street.
There's a Mexican club where the dancers are silhouetted
against floor-to-ceiling windows. Tag thinks it looks fun. I
say it's a bit crass. He sighs.

I say: 'Maybe my sister's right. I've become a hard bitch.'

'You are, but I think I'm softening you.'

'And I'm certainly softening you. More's the pity.'

'Can't you let up for one minute, Nina?'

'Is it all too much, coming from a mother of two? Would
you rather I was sitting here in a nursing bra splurting milk
everywhere, or leaning across to wipe your mouth with
the edge of my napkin?' He doesn't know what to say.
'What is it with you, Tag? Why can't you loosen up and
have fun?'

'I don't have the time for that sort of fun. I've got a career
to sort out. You don't realise it, Nina, but 99 per cent of my
free time is devoted to you.'

I say: 'I need to feel wanted and sexy; not interesting but
unsuitable.'

'Your problem, Nina, is you feel that Buster still has a
hold over you because, technically, he's still your husband. I was the same after Jay, remember? I cringe at
the clinches I got myself into after he left. I was a lot
wiser second time around – maybe because *I* made the
decision to end it.' Mala stops for a moment and retouches
her lipstick. 'When the divorce comes through, you'll shed
Buster like an old skin. Rag, Tag and Bobtail: none of this

will matter. Trust me.' I slump into a chair. Mala says: 'I was talking to a woman about aphrodisiacs. She says the only real aphrodisiac is a new partner. That's why you're hot.'

Yeah. I'm horny: horny horny horny.

'Mummy, what's Christine like?'

'I don't know, Darling.'

'Daddy wants us to meet her.'

'You will, Sweetheart. At some point.'

'Is she pretty?'

'You've seen her picture.'

'She *is* pretty.' Lilla changes the outfit on her Cabbage Patch Doll. 'Do you think she's nice Mummy?'

I turn away from her. I say: 'Darling, I've told you. Your father is a lovely man. He's kind and he's funny and he's got a good heart. I don't believe he would love someone who wasn't as nice as him.'

'Welcome back, Nina. Everyone's thrilled that you're here.' Eric Casey motions me to take a seat. Black leather and chrome. 'Coffee? Hot, sweet and black, as I recall. Jane, can you see to that?' He presses a button and blinds swish across the windows overlooking St James's Square. In the corner his male assistant turns on the slide projector and a number of fashion mastheads suddenly flash on to the blank white wall.

'Now, Nina, this is the group of catalogues with which we're having particular trouble. We've done two mailshots in the past six months. The product is top-notch, but somewhere along the line we're getting the mix wrong. The uptake has been relatively small.' A table of figures now replaces the colourful mish-mash. 'These show projected sales against actual sales. As you can see, similar ranges are selling almost twice as much. Naturally, our clients are getting anxious. What we want *you* to do, is overhaul the whole project.'

'I'll need to be talked through the products.'

'A designer's coming in on Wednesday to explain the difference between a revere and a Nehru collar.'

'Who's on the team?'

'Carmen Mmono, who's been working on car accounts for the Sunday supps, and Chris DeFries who's fresh to the job but has a wonderful turn of phrase. Axel Manley has commissioned Faith Hargreaves to do the snaps and the conference suite is booked for two days in week three for your team to bash through the details.' He smiles. 'How does that sound?'

I remain cool though my heart is pounding through the silk of my new shirt: 'It's pushing it, Eric, but we'll manage, I'm sure.'

'I can't be bothered with these phone calls, Tag. They bore me.'

'What are you saying?'

'It's over. Finito.'

'You're ending our friendship?'

'This isn't a friendship. This is a co-dependent counselling service that's lasted half a lifetime. I'm cutting loose.'

'But we have feelings for each other.'

'Lots of feelings, no feel*ing*. I'm fed up with it.'

'Let's meet and talk.'

'There's nothing left to say. I adore you, but you're like a beauty spot. A pleasant decoration of little actual use.'

'That's an appalling thing to say.'

'I'm pre-menstrual.'

'Call me back when the bleeding's over.'

'I've done all my bleeding over you, Tag. Goodbye.'

Turkey night. There's a buzz around the table; giggles and

gossip. We are ten in all: Maddie, Mala, Liz and Laura. Caroline and Jan, who's back in town for a few days; Cathy from BCAF and two dear friends from way back. Mala has pinned me into a black veil with a Kite-mark Sellotaped on the back. 'It's to show you're tried and tested, Nina.'

'Tried, tested and failed. Not quite the same thing.'

'It's Buster who's failed. Wear your badge with pride.'

Jan says: 'Have *you* got a badge now: Assistant Editor?'

Maddie calls up the table: 'Any objections to my ordering the wine?' The spiky-haired waiter ignores our appreciative glances as she talks him through the choices. 'Do we want champagne?'

Cathy says: 'We're fizzing enough without it.' She lowers her voice: 'Don't bother giving him the eye, Nina. They're virtually all gay in the Groucho.'

A packet of cream-filled chocolate willies materialises. Liz opens it and groans: 'Only six. That's about half a willie each.'

'Half a willie is better than none.'

'It depends which half, Janice.'

'I've started work, Buster.'

'Let me know when you get paid so I can reduce my contribution.'

'If you reduce it quickly there's no incentive for me to continue. I need to get ahead of myself. The kids' new shoes came to £76 and Lilla's piano lessons are £15 a week.'

'We can talk about that when you produce the figures, Nina. I'm on the verge of bankruptcy.'

'We are no longer married – I have no obligation to keep *you*.'

'I've been semi-dependent for years. You can't change someone's life overnight and expect them to recover in minutes. I'm doing bloody well; don't derail me.'

'Make sure you keep doing well. I don't have to be this generous. I could have forced you to sell the house.'

'Have you no moral conscience, Buster?'

'We're not talking about morals, we're talking about the law.'

Liz makes the toast: 'To Nina, whose spirit is undimmed. Health, wealth and happiness.' The others cheer.

Laura says: 'If we do this again in five years' time, I wonder how many of our marriages will still be intact?'

'Mine will last,' Cathy says. 'I've made the right choice.'

'Lucky you.'

Pleased, she says: 'Richard's first wife wouldn't sleep with him for the last four years of their marriage. I don't know why he stayed – but I guess that's Richard for you: loyal, loving, steady. I'm so glad I met him.'

Maddie winces: 'Sex isn't everything in the long term.'

Cathy shrugs: 'The most time you spend with them is in bed, isn't it? I mean – when you're working, you barely see each other. If there's no action between the sheets, you're wasting eight precious hours together. Think of that.'

We all do.

Laura says: 'Wait till you've got children. You'll be continually exhausted. Wait until your eight precious hours is reduced to five. It won't be so clear cut then.'

Maddie says: 'It's shared responsibilities that bind you.'

Caroline tips back her head and blows out a perfect nicotined O. 'It isn't that important to the *wives*. I meet married men every day who're desperate for affairs. Don't be fooled when your husbands lose interest in sex – it just means they're looking elsewhere.'

Later, Maddie will say: 'That evening, I knew. I saw what my relationship with Gavin had become: emotionally sterile. It isn't enough to enjoy browsing in Richard Dare or Harvey

Nicks. Our children aren't enough. I didn't see that before. I suddenly felt that if I didn't go back and shake up our lives, we were heading for oblivion.'

Oblivion: the condition of being forgotten or disregarded.

Jan says: 'Do you sleep with married men, Caroline?'

Caroline looks at her coldly: 'That is a typical Janice question.'

'What's the answer?'

They size each other up across the table. Caroline says: 'My private life is my own affair. If I answer "no", I'm giving you an insight into the way I make decisions; and if I say "yes" you'll use that to construct an argument against me.'

'You just seem such an expert, that's all.'

'One can recognise and place a chair without sitting on it.'

'I haven't forgotten, Nina.'

'So why can't you come?'

'I've a case in Newcastle that day. I'll see him at the weekend.'

'It's his fourth birthday, Buster! You've always been there.'

'I can't change it. I'll call.'

We share out empty bottles – wine and hideous Hildon water – and make harmonious music by blowing across the tops. Other diners look charily in our direction. This makes us laugh.

Laura says: 'Isn't it brilliant being out in a big group of women? I'd forgotten how . . . intimate it all gets.'

Mala says: 'You mean a group of big women.'

Liz whispers: 'And the word isn't "intimate", it's "dirty".'

Laura peers at her over a glass: 'We marrieds prefer "intimate".'

'Because it elevates the notion of sexuality?'
'No, Mala, because it brings love into it.'
'That's what I meant.' Mala grins and we all laugh.
Cathy says drunkenly: 'Sex with love is a hundred times more intimate than without.'
I say, 'Yes. It is. But it isn't half as much fun.'
Mala groans: 'Why are we still talking about men?' The waiter surveys her coldly. She winks: 'Maybe you could remind me?'
'I don't think my boyfriend would like that.'
The giggling comes back round the table like a Mexican wave.

September fifteenth. Jack's birthday. There's no card from Buster. His present from us both is a Lego construction set. He's happy. I pop thirty Penguins into a bag for him to share with his class. Lilla says: 'Has Daddy rung?' I shake my head. She looks upset. I bundle them into the car: 'Come on, or we'll be late.'

I take a half day, coming home at two to prepare the party: the waxed paper tablecloth covered in dalmatians; twelve matching cups and plates; a Superman cake made by my mother. She says: 'Has Buster rung?' I shake my head.

Three twenty, I go to collect the children. Jack is so excited he keeps shouting and jumping. We rush home. Laura's two oldest are dropped off almost immediately. Maddie and the twins call to say they're leaving: 'I've made chicken sandwiches and chocolate drop cakes; I'm also bringing homemade lemonade so they don't have to drink that ghastly shop stuff.' The doorbell goes. Two small bodies are hurriedly thrust into the hallway. More rings, more children.

Lilla says: 'Has Daddy rung?' I shake my head.

At four thirty, the magician arrives and sets up in the sitting room while the kids excitedly pass the parcel in the kitchen. At five, he does a one-hour show and Mum, Maddie and I drink tea. As I refill the pot, Buster's parents arrive. At six, the hungry kids troop back into the kitchen and demolish the food. A bowl of crisps is upended and one child claims Twiglets make her sick. Laura's younger boy refuses to eat a thing. Stash pretends he has a machine gun and massacres his fellow guests. Maddie's two talk to each other in silly voices. Jack wails: 'I want my Daddy!'

Lilla says: 'Has Daddy rung?' I shake my head.

At six thirty, parents arrive to remove their offspring.

At seven, Maddie goes.

At seven thirty, Buster's parents leave.

Mum and I put the children to bed.

At eight o'clock the phone rings. I answer it in my bedroom: 'Nina, it's me. I'm so sorry I couldn't ring earlier. We had a terrible day in court – nothing went as planned. We've had to completely rethink our line on the case. The meeting's only just finished. Did Jack have a good day?'

'Yes, Buster, a brilliant day.'

'Will you put him on the phone?'

'He's in bed.' I go into Jack's room. He is fast asleep with a Beany Baby leopard in his arms.

Buster says: 'Oh God, I'm so sorry. I tried my damndest, honestly. Will you tell him I'm sorry? I'll make a point of ringing before he goes to school in the morning.'

I say: 'Fine.'

Lilla calls from her bed: 'Was that Daddy?'

'Yes.'

'He never said Happy Birthday to Jack.'

'He was busy. He got caught up on a case.'

'He's always busy.'

I go into her room and hug her. I push back her thick fringe and kiss her forehead. She puts trusting arms around my neck and pulls me to her: 'I love you so much, Mummy.'

*   *   *

As we sort out the bill, Mala says: 'Let's have a final toast for Nina and her bunch of ageing slappers.'

'Speak for yourself,' Cathy snorts.

Laura shakes her head: 'I give thanks I'm married. Who'd want a short-sighted woman with three children?'

'Tut tut: you've not been reading our Woman's Page. Ready-made families are the new thing. Instant parenthood, half the responsibility. You're freed up to lie in bed and make lurve every other weekend. It's a pretty good deal.'

'So they're queueing up for you, are they, Mala?'

'I'd like to think so, Caroline, but I'm not available. Twice bitten—'

Jan says: 'Third time lucky.'

Cathy squeals: 'Don't be daft! If she couldn't get it right before, why should she pull it off now?'

Maddie says stiffly: 'Perhaps you should ask your new husband that?'

Clearing out a drawer, I come across the card Buster gave me the Christmas before he fell in love with Christine. 'To the source of all bliss. Love you for ever, Darling.'

'Hello Nina, how's it going?'

'Paul. Very well.'

'I heard much raucous laughter when I passed your office this morning.'

'Carmen was suggesting that a point in favour of satin knickers is they slip off more quickly.'

'That's certainly a selling consideration.'

'Except they go up to a size 32. My argument was that once we lard out, getting out of any knickers becomes a bit of a struggle.'

Nonplussed he says: 'Yes, I suppose so.'

'For example, if we tried to recreate the lift scene from

Fatal Attraction right now, we'd be at the top floor before you got your fingers in my waistband.'

Paul blanches.

At the second floor, Danny Jacobson gets in: 'I just met Carmen Mmono in the canteen – I've ordered twenty pairs of satin knickers for the wife.'

'So you can ravish her more easily?'

'After thirty years? Of course not. She needs replacement J-Cloths.'

As we get closer to an agreement, my ex-husband starts inspecting the way I spend money. He comments on new clothes and CDs. I say: 'I don't have the same freedom to wander round your new premises clocking your purchases, Buster. Drop it.'

He grins sweetly; Busterly. I think of the Christmas card. I say: 'What went wrong?'

He's still smiling. 'You're always asking.'

'And you're never telling.'

When Maddie pops round later the kids are watching MTV. She says: 'What is that racket?'

'Well it isn't the song of the whale.'

'Don't put me down, Nina.'

'Oh, is it only allowed when you're dishing out?'

Suddenly I notice tears pouring down her face. I'm immediately distressed. 'What is it, Maddie? What's wrong?'

She says: 'I don't know. I think Gavin and I are in crisis.'

'You should slow down, Mala. Pace yourself.'

'You can't pace yourself on a newspaper, Nina. We're re-active, not proactive. Anyway, you're a fine one to talk.' She holds up a floral Liberty chiffon: 'Is this the sort of thing you're talking about?'

I hold it to the light: 'Yes. It's very difficult. Our clients basically change the patterns and colours just enough to get away with copying, but I keep worrying. It's custom and practice I suppose – I've just got to learn the tricks.'

We continue checking out the endless rolls of material that make up just one small section of the store. Before we leave, I put together a small folder of swatches. Outside, I say: 'It's been a privilege to have an hour of your company.'

'It *has*. It's just me and the dep ed running the show this week. The head honcho claims to have ME. God help us all. The children have barely seen me. They'll be suing for neglect.'

'Ah, the vagaries of modern single-parenthood.'

I know Maddie's in a bad way because she doesn't say anything when I make processed ham sandwiches for the children. She is sitting at the kitchen table where we've shared so much sadness in recent times, and now it is her who is bowed under an invisible cosh. I gather the children and bribe them to play upstairs. 'So what's going on?'

'I don't know. If I did, it wouldn't seem so terrible.'

'There isn't someone else?'

'For Gavin? No.'

'And you?'

She looks up, surprised. 'Of course not.'

Cashing in on her diminished rigour, I make her tea using a teabag. 'So tell me.'

'There's nothing to tell.'

'Then why are you crying?' I want to put an arm around her, but Maddie's always uncomfortable with physical contact. She squirms as if it puts her under some sort of emotional obligation. Instead I sit next to her, elbows touching.

She says: 'I just feel we can't carry on the way we are.'

'Is it just you who feels this?'

'Gavin doesn't think about anything but work. As long as everything's as it should be, he's happy.'

'And you're not?'

'I don't know. I was devising a new honey mayonnaise and it suddenly came to me that my life was empty.' She gestures around the room: 'You're so alive at the moment, Nina. You're always going out; doing things. What do I do?'

'You're married.' I jump up: 'Let's go out and get plastered. I'll ask Mum to babysit.'

'Is that your answer to everything?'

'It's fun, it helps; it's occasional.' I massage her tensed shoulders; she stiffens. 'You see, Maddie, you'd hate my life. You don't enjoy partying and flirting and playing silly buggers – you never have. Even as kids, I listened to records and you locked yourself away to do extra homework.'

A marriage break-up doesn't *change* the obsessions and attitudes of women – it *restores* them. Thus the livewire is restored as a livewire. But the gentle wallflower will still be a gentle wallflower.

Axel flicks a light so I can study the transparencies with a magnifier. I make a face. He says: 'Not bad, huh?'

'Not bad for pleated chiffon and a *faux* Versace neck scarf.'

He pulls a bottle of Black Label from a shelf: 'Small drink?' We toast each other: future success. He pecks me on the cheek: 'It's great having you back. Don't leave again.'

'I'm only here till Christmas.'

'Because Eric was worried you might have lost it. You haven't. Wait and see – there'll be a job at the end.'

'I'm not sure that's what I want.'

'Plenty of time to think about it. Anyway you'd miss me.' I blow him a kiss. He catches it in his hand: 'Mutual admiration: a good start. Talking of which, are you ready to hear my spiel?'

It's half past seven on a Friday night and we're making our first conference presentation on the Monday morning. As Axel pulls out the mock-ups and charts, I put down my glass and collapse in one of the leather client chairs. 'God, I'm exhausted; and it's only been three weeks.'

'Mummy, I miss you.'

'I know, Lovely. But it's good for all of us that I'm working.'

'Why is it good for me and Jack?'

'Because I can pay for all the little things we need.'

'I'd rather have *you*.'

'It's good for me to get out, Lilla. You're at school in the day, I'm at work. I'd be lonely if I were in the house on my own.'

'You were on your own when Daddy was here.'

'And I was getting bored. This is good for me and good for you. I'm a much more interesting person.'

'How?'

We stare blankly at each other and then laugh.

Will has issued Mala and me with invitations to a publisher's rock 'n' roll party at the Royal College of Art. It's Wednesday night. She arrives straight from work looking wonderful in a chocolate-brown Agnès B trouser-suit and stunning Allie Connors' jewellery, but she's rubbing her eyes as we enter the building: 'I've put the paper to bed the past three nights. Home by one and back for morning conference at ten.'

'That's eight hours' sleeping and one hour's travel.'

'That's five hours sleeping, ninety minutes horsing with the kids, thirty minutes getting ready, ninety minutes trawling the papers back to front and thirty minutes in a cab.'

'Very impressive. If you don't become an editor, you could earn a fortune devising train timetables.'

'Or sizing bras – if you give me a job on your team, that is.'

Music is wafting down the corridor as we edge our way into a vast room filled with red American fridges. Like Alice entering the looking glass, we tempt fate and open one. It's full of beer. Mala closes the door and rearranges the magnetic letters left there: RIP.

'Who's died?'

'Rock 'n' roll by the sound of it. Where's the stage? Stephen King's playing tonight.'

'The horror writer?'

'Yes. Watch out, Nina, or you might end up with rats in the belfry and a hatchet through your head.' She stops and swivels in the opposite direction: 'On the other hand, given the bloody politicking at work, maybe I'm the one who'll be spooked. It's a bunfight. The ed's still off sick. Word is, he's about to be fired. We're all running round like headless chickens.' As she muscles a group of young men out of the way, a voice says: 'Mala Fonseka!'

Mala turns and squeals with delight: 'Letty!' They hug. 'Nina, Letty was my editor on *Romantic Love*. Two old bags left on the grouchy shelf of life.' She lifts Letty's left hand and shows me the most enormous rock. 'Mind you, she's fallen on her feet in a big way. A small-time baronet with a humungous legacy.' Behind us King begins a solo on the makeshift stage. Mala says: 'How many books do you have to sell to get a party like this?'

'Over a million.'

'I'll never get a gig then.'

'What do you play?'
'At the moment? Second fiddle.'

Liz says: 'Nina, it's my friend's wedding this Saturday. Will you come with me? I can't bear the prospect of everyone asking why I haven't tied the knot.'
'Do you care?'
'Of course I care. Doesn't every woman want to settle down in the end?'

Hey rock 'n'roll. In the mêlée, Will gives a wave. Behind us, two new authors are discussing their first novels; the one I vaguely recognise from a newspaper feature, has clocked up twenty thousand orders. The other, a small-time broadcaster, is listening intently to his every word.

I try and eavesdrop. She is saying: 'You must be *so* thrilled.'

He looks uncertain: 'They haven't actually been sold yet.'

Mala says: 'This is Daniel Monk, marketing manager of Henriques Dudley. He's the one who stage-managed my book.'

A gracious greying man in a well cut suit, he smiles: 'And what stage of romantic love are you at, Nina?'

'Both the end and the beginning.'

There's a twinkle in his eye. 'Ah, a victim of the current epidemic? Clearly nobody followed your advice, Mala.'

'Don't tell me you've joined the club?'

He laughs: 'If only my wife would let me.' Looking into the middle distance he is suddenly distracted. 'I've just seen Lawrie Grimes – he's got a brilliant new novel coming out in January – we'll give you an exclusive if you promise a decent spread, Mala.'

'What's new about him?'

'The hero of his book is a Freddy Kruger for the Millennium.'

'Film rights sold?'

'Under negotiation. I'll send you a proof.' Momentarily, Daniel's attention returns to me. 'Perhaps you should meet him, Nina. Like you, he's a bit lost and found at the moment.'

Lost and found: a slip of the tongue.

I am lost without Buster. I have lost my sense of time. He was the one who declared himself an existentialist, but I am the one who's been left with only a sense of 'now'. My long-term goals are uncertain. Only the wish to be happy is fixed. The fretwork of my life, which set out in exact detail my course from square to square, has been replaced by a web where all directions are possible. I have lost my sense of place. My behaviour is erratic: veering from wild and girlish to severe and motherly. I feel hard. I say things I shouldn't; I have inappropriate thoughts for a woman my age; I misread social cues. I have no listing in the catalogue: the one-line description that says married woman or single girl. I am neither of these. I am *just* a woman.

Buster left me to find space, but immediately moved into someone else's. For the first time in years, I truly have it. It doesn't matter that the children inhabit it with me. We are an intrinsic part of each other. Before, my contentment came from making Buster and the kids happy; it was *sensed* rather than experienced: I had achieved what I wanted for the family. Now I actually *feel* content. I am relaxed; sunny: happy. Happy being me.

Whoever me is.

Liz and I bask in the warm autumn sun. From around the back of the church, a 1959 fin-tailed Cadillac crunches into view. The bride, in lilac, and groom, in matching brocade waistcoat, hop inside. We lob confetti and follow the bridal procession into the grounds of the local manor house. Champagne is flowing on the lawn. The photographs take nearly two hours. We decamp for the wedding lunch in the cobbled courtyard at the back. Linen and lanterns, bunting and balloons. A little boy with a seating list places me next to a couple I vaguely know through Liz. The woman says: 'We were so sorry to hear about your break-up.'

'That's very kind of you.'

'How are the children?'

'They're doing very well.'

'And you? You look fantastic!' Behind the eyes, she's blank.

I say: 'Every cloud—'

'But it must have been such a shock! Buster Goodholme – champion of the underdog: of all people. You must feel so bitter.'

'Not really. Ultimately, it's Buster who'll pay the price.'

'Because you're going to hit him for every penny you can get!'

'Because he's lost his family.' I turn away crossly.

'Do you think *this* marriage will last?'

'I hope so. If a perfect wedding is any indication, they're on the road to marital bliss.'

'Wasn't yours a perfect wedding?'

'Not really. It rained. We couldn't have the hood down on our wedding car. My hair was a mess and my heels kept sinking into the turf. I'm leaning at an angle of forty-five degrees in most of the photos. In retrospect, I don't suppose it augured well.'

She smirks at me: 'I suppose the biggest indication of things going wrong was the fact you married Buster?'

I say: 'There was nothing wrong with my marrying Buster. At least he didn't shag every girl in his office like the man sitting by *your* side.'

*   *   *

Lawrie Grimes virtually ignores me, but he's camply cap-
tivated by Mala. He circles her like an exhibit: 'You're
extraordinary. A fantasy houri.'

'Watch your language.'

He gazes at her adoringly: 'Who are you?'

Daniel Monk makes the introductions; delighted. On
discovering the object of his affections is an acting deputy
editor, Lawrie gushes even more. Mala starts to enjoy
the attention. I say to Daniel: 'He's very flamboyant for
a writer.'

'Not cast in the usual mould, certainly. His family are
circus people; he has the showman in him.' Lawrie is
whispering in Mala's ear and she is laughing. 'He still
performs, actually.'

'And he writes well?'

'He has a gift for putting the willies up people.'

'Well, Mala could certainly do with a bit of that.'

Two a.m. We're driving through central London after the
wedding.

Liz says: 'So are you carrying on the list or starting again
from zero?'

'What list?'

'The hit list.'

'What hit list?' Red traffic lights. Euston Road.

'When we were single and hitting the hotspots of London
NW3, you used to keep a list of all the men you'd slept
with.' Oh. 'Are you adding to it, or starting with a clean
page?'

'I've only slept with one man since Buster left.'

'That wasn't the question.'

I skid-start in the direction of the underpass. Bloody
rain. From the back, an unnamed guest we're returning
to Camden, asks: 'How many were you up to?'

'How many what?'

'How many men? To keep a list, you must have been counting.'

'Why would I tell you?'

'Because I'm a stranger. It might help.'

He makes us laugh. I say: 'What does it matter? It's all talk at our age anyway. The hunt's far more fun than the kill.'

Liz stifles a yawn. 'Wasn't it ever thus?'

'I can't remember.'

'And you can't remember the number either? *Very* convenient.'

I say: 'Put it this way: I was effectively a virgin for ten years. That means I start with a clean page. Is that good enough for the two of you?'

Lilla is on the phone to Buster, treating him alternately with affection and contempt. As usual. Jack has said he can't be bothered to get up off the sofa and say hello. As usual.

Lilla says: 'Daddy, what time will you come and see us on Thursday?' They have a long talk about absolutely nothing. She has learned the trick of speaking without stopping long enough for him to respond. For several minutes she seamlessly spins together a number of equally meaningless anecdotes, questions, opinions and strange noises.

When Buster calls on his mobile phone I imagine his distress as the bill mounts and his daughter refuses to stop: 'All right Daddy, I *will* finish – but just let me tell you this one thing.' Half of the prattle borders on the abusive. It makes me laugh.

Tonight she's planning ahead. Half term is three weeks away and Buster's promised to take Lilla and Jack out of London for two days. Her stream of consciousness takes in cottages and caravans, Wales and Cornwall, Burger King and the Happy Eater. She tells him about her lunch at my mother's place, and the kazoo that Jack was given by one of the neighbours. As she reaches the end she pauses only momentarily. I imagine him gathering breath at the other end, ready to answer all her little queries. Lilla doesn't wait. Finishing with a flourish she says: 'I'd better go now, Dad. I've things to do.' She slams down the phone – 'I love that man' – and goes to watch TV with Jack.

Since Buster has had the children alternate weekends, they have visited virtually every pleasure palace known to man: places he refused to visit as a family because of time, cost and crowds. They're the most envied children in their schools. They have new toys and endless sweets. At handover time, they are blissed out: and I am the devil incarnate. I make them brush their teeth. I make them go to bed. Lilla has to do little bits of homework. She stomps up the stairs angrily: 'You're horrid, Mum! I hate you!'

Jack follows, kicking the skirting: 'And I hate you too, Mummy.'

I bring up the rear; resigned. 'Thank you for that, children. Can we head towards the bathroom now, do you think?'

When I see Maddie again, she looks drawn; thin. I sit in her kitchen shelling peas while she makes chicken stock. Even with the windows open, the house heaves with the smell of boiling giblets. The boys are out with Susannah; Gavin has some problem at work. The roof of the Millennium Dome is complete; the internal sections are being constructed, but the religious slot remains worryingly unclaimed. Does this mean that God is dead or is it simply that we've given up the ghost? The Holy Ghost.

The house is silent but for the sound of Maddie chopping vegetables manically with a Chinese cleaver.

I work silently. Finally she says: 'I don't know why I feel like this.' I nod. 'It's not as if he's done anything wrong or

said something to upset me. It's just that there's a great gap
and I don't know what's supposed to go into it.' She oils
and heats the wok while seasoning the mish-mash. 'Maybe
it's my time of life. Maybe because the boys are at school.
I don't know. My work's fine. His work's fine. We run this
place like a business. We need –' she sets a clock to time
her cooking and tips in the veg, 'for nothing. So what's
wrong?' Still I sit. Maddie turns and faces me, her cheeks
steamed red from the pot. 'I just feel so empty. I feel like
I don't know where I'm going. Or even, who with.'

I don't know what to say. I hand her the full bowl of
shelled peas. She pops them in a freezer bag and stores
them. 'Do you want a tea?' She puts the kettle on, pulls out
a Bodum glass teapot and looks through a set of Fortnum &
Mason loose-leaf boxes. 'You don't like the smell of Chinese
do you? Too smoky.' She is talking to herself.

Lilla says: 'Is it true we're having tea with Christine?'
'Yes. Daddy's going to take you on Sunday.'
'Oh goody!' I turn away so she can't see my face. She
says: 'What will it be like, Mummy?'
I say: 'It'll be fine. She wants to be your friend. If you be
good, it'll be easy all round.'
'Why can't we spend a weekend with her?'
'Because it's too early.'
'Daddy doesn't think so.'
'Daddy doesn't *think*.'

Maddie brings the tea to the table. I say: 'If Gavin's not the
problem, it must be you.'
'He *may* be the problem.' She pours into plain Conran
shop cups. 'I just don't know.'
'Can you pinpoint when you started feeling like this?'
'I know exactly when: it was your bloody marriage
ending!' I ignore the accusatory tone and wait. She says: 'It

made me see that you can't take anything for granted. I've always assumed that Gavin and I were perfectly matched – but perhaps we're not.'

'You think this, because Buster ran off with another woman? It doesn't make sense, Madeline.'

'Don't call me that.'

I sip my tea. 'Let's talk it through before blaming Gavin.'

'I'm not blaming Gavin.'

'But you will. Trawl back, Mads. Just before Buster went, your book on dishes around the world was junked because the fashion's for single-theme cookbooks. That meant you had to give up on your plan for a conservatory.' She gets up and gives the contents of the wok a vigorous stir. 'It also meant you'd missed the boat in terms of getting something out in time for Christmas.'

'What point are you making, Nina?'

'Now Mala's sacked Sebastian Wilkie and employed Jennifer Craft as your main newspaper rival, the heat's on in the kitchen.'

The lid goes back on. 'I don't care about Jennifer Craft.'

'Yes you do, Maddie. You care more about your cooking than anything else. Right now, things aren't going to plan – and you're taking it out on Gavin.'

'Gavin doesn't know I feel like this!'

'And you're not going to tell him are you? *Are* you? That way you can feel angry with him for not noticing. You can hate *him* instead of hating your editor or Jennifer Craft or whoever it is that's really causing your unhappiness.'

'This is cod psychology, Nina.'

'Don't make Gavin the scapegoat. You saw what happened to me. Don't bring that on yourself, Maddie.'

'Was it nice having tea with Christine?'

'Lovely.'

'Did you behave yourselves?'

Bored: 'Yes, Mum.'

On the floor are the Tiny Tears and Action Man that Buster bought the children on the way to meet his paramour. Pasta and chocolate eclairs; videos and games. A wonderful end to an active weekend with Daddy. I pace the bathroom, steadily getting wetter from Jack and Lilla's splashing. I want to ask more, but not the kind of enquiries children can process: do you think, when Christine saw you so fresh and innocent, she regretted breaking up your lives for her own ends? I say nothing. They say nothing.

By the time I put them to bed, I'm surprised to find we've moved on to other things.

'How did it go?'

'Very well. The children liked her. She gave them nice food and mixed orange juice so Lilla's doll did proper-looking pees.'

'They're bound to like her to begin with. What about later?'

'There's no point worrying.'

'You're being very philosophical, Nina.'

'I don't have a choice. If I die tomorrow, she takes charge. Think about it, Laura. Life goes on.'

One call ends, another begins. My mother says: 'If you ignore the subject, it won't just go away. She's steadily going to become a feature of their lives.'

'If I ignore her, it makes *me* feel better.'

'If you ignore her, she'll feel she can do whatever she likes with *your* children.'

'Well she can pretty much, can't she? But I'm here as their base line, when they come home. That's all that matters.'

A man with whom I swapped numbers at the Villa Stefano phones me at work. His voice, like his cheeky face, turns me

weak at the knees. Within minutes of our setting eyes on
each other, he'd handed me his business card and asked me
to call. I wrote my own number on the back and returned
it: 'If you want to talk to me, *you* call.'

He's a businessman; a wide-boy flying by the seat of his
pants. He makes me laugh. He tells me I'm sexy. I want to
see him. We meet for lunch the next day.

Lawrie Grimes makes a dinner date with Mala. 'I'm so
bloody busy, I can't see him till next week.'

'Playing hard to get?'

'I *am* hard to get at the moment.'

'Isn't he a bit . . . theatrical?'

'He's a maverick, Nina. All you see is his image. There's
a bloody good brain underneath the bluster.'

'And Josh?'

'Nothing is going on between me and Josh.'

'And it could between you and Lawrie? He isn't your
type, Mala.'

'You're just jealous.'

'Maybe I am. Not of Lawrie: of you. If you get hooked
on someone, I'll lose my best going-out buddy.'

Wide-boy is twice divorced with two children.

He leads an incredibly complex life. He works late into the
night, ringing as he drives between appointments. We talk a
lot and steal away for lunches which end in long kisses.

One Friday night he calls late at my door. We stay awake
till six, snuggled up on the sofa; gentle, loving, chastely
turning each other on. Every touch, every flutter, has an
effect on him. He says: 'You free me inside.'

More is impossible. Upstairs, two small children are safe
and warm in their beds. He has custody of his sons: same
problem. His mother is babysitting overnight. Neither of us
is free to bring someone back.

I say: 'What we both need is partners with no kids and their own homes.'

Later, I take Jack and Lilla to see *Mulan* so I can have a doze in the Warner Village cinema. And I suddenly understand why young mothers, desperate for company and comfort, risk leaving children alone at home while they slip off to see friends or have a drink. I see how those horrible accidents where something happens to an untended child, come about. It is a scenario in which every player from the adult down is suffering from neglect.

Solitude is a gift: but it can only be enjoyed if it's snatched or earned. Long-term solitude, especially when imposed by circumstances beyond our control, has another name. A sadder name. Loneliness.

Maddie unexpectedly picks me up from work: 'I've got such brilliant news – I wanted to tell you in person.'

Inexplicably, I'm worried. 'What kind of news?'

She's grinning fit to burst: 'I'm getting my own TV series!' Seeing my confusion she says: 'They approached me months ago with an idea. I said yes – because everyone cooks on TV now – but then it went silent. I thought it was because there was too much audience participation, but this morning I got the call: we start work next week!'

Still uncertain, I say: 'I'm so pleased for you, Mads!'

'I know. Isn't it wonderful? I'm going to be rushed off my feet doing a column as well, but I'm so happy!'

'What about Gavin?'

'*What* about Gavin?'

'Is everything all right?'

'Oh he's doing brilliantly – you know that.'

'I mean, how are things between the two of you?' Now *she* looks confused. I say: 'For God's sake, Maddie, only a couple of weeks ago, you didn't know if you had a marriage.'

'Oh we're absolutely fine.'

'So the crisis is over?'

'The crisis? Yes, of course.'

'How did you resolve things? In your own mind, I mean.'

'Well, they've sort of resolved themselves, haven't they Nina? I mean we're both focused and busy. The children are thriving at school. What more does either of us need?'

Wide-boy's hands are inside my sweatshirt, keeping warm as much as inspecting the contents. It's three a.m. and we're on Primrose Hill looking across London to the Telecom Tower and the old Capital Radio building. Across to the left, flashing intermittently in the mist, is the pyramid on top of Canary Wharf. The city is still half lit. It's beautiful.

I run my nails lightly up and down his back. It's so quiet; peaceful. Occasionally cars skim past on the roads below us; circling both the hill and the northern boundary of Regent's Park, the netted peaks of the Snowdon aviary like Toblerones in the dark. He says: 'I'm falling for you. You know that.'

'But we can't carry on like this.'

'Why not?'

'Because we've nowhere to go. It's mid-October. Almost winter. I'm getting hypothermia out here.' We hold each other tightly. More tightly. Out of the corner of my eye I see two men in the trees below us, doing up their flies.

I say: 'This is no way for a mother of two to be spending time.'

Too much work, too many late nights, too little patience for the demands of small children.

It's bedtime and I've had enough. Lilla demands a tape; Jack won't settle. I am on the landing screaming at them. Hurling abuse. Saying cruel and hurtful things.

Lilla dashes at me in anger. I pull her hair so hard, I'm

surprised it doesn't come off in my hand. She holds her head in pain and disbelief and starts to howl.

I see Jack watching from his bedroom door. I approach him in a fury to get him back to bed. Terrified, he launches himself into the duvet. I stand there not knowing what to do. My daughter's distress is overwhelming. And all I want to do is go somewhere quiet and be me.

As the howls become despairing sobs and she waits for me to somehow make it right, I go into my bedroom and shut the door; cutting myself off from the self-created horror outside.

Mala rings me up: 'I'm seeing Lawrie tonight.'

'Ah yes, the gap in your time frame.'

'I'm knackered. I've aged ten years in recent weeks. He's taking me to the River Café.'

'He must have got a big advance?'

'Six figures. What should I wear?'

'Wear something cream and low: flaunt what you've got.'

'They're like empty icing bags since I had kids.'

'He might be into cake decoration.'

'I'll take along some hundreds and thousands then.'

'Sounds like he's already got hundreds and thousands, Mala. You'll have to be the jam in his sponge.'

Paul Avedon wanders awkwardly into my office. 'Nina, I'm chairing the ALMC Awards next month: November thirteenth. I'm top table and everyone's in couples.' I smile up at him and wait. 'As you probably know, it's months since my last liaison spluttered out. I wondered, if it's not too much of an imposition, if you'd be my partner for the evening?'

Mala rings at one a.m. 'I just had to talk to someone.'

'You're alone, I take it?'

'Just got back. God, Nina – he's wonderful.'

'Is that why you're breaking your own rule?'

'What rule?'

'The I-never-get-it-right-so-I've-had-it-with-men rule.'

'Did I say that?'

'Two years ago when you booted Cal out.'

'And I've stuck to it.'

'Precisely. So what is it about Lawrie Grimes that's enticed you into the water?'

'He's just awash with words, Nina. Full of passion. We didn't stop talking all night. He's been everywhere – done everything. You know he's a journalist too – writes for *The New Yorker*.'

I smile in my semi-sleep: 'Mala despite the fact that I've got a breakfast meeting with Eric Casey, I am delighted you have chosen to share this with me.'

'Are you being rude?'

'No: I'm congratulating you, you jammy cow! Is the feeling mutual?'

'He said I was the most exciting woman he'd met in years.'

'That's certainly true. How many marriages?'

'None. Seven live-in lovers; five engagements.'

'Five engagements!' I'm wide awake. 'This is a man without an ounce of judgement! Ditch him Mala, don't waste your time.'

'Nina, all we've done is break bread together.'

'Well don't let him put any buns in your oven.'

'You're doing brilliantly, Nina.'

'It's only the first part of the project.'

'Even so.' Eric Casey, gets up and looks out on to an overcase city afternoon. 'You must be wondering why BCAF has spent two years aggressively chasing below-the-line accounts?'

'It's certainly not as glamorous or as lucrative as the big stuff.'

'But if you think in terms of a large consultancy putting companies on their feet in return for, say, a percentage of gross sales, it's far more attractive. You understand what I'm saying?'

'Very clearly.'

'Also, these accounts are in areas which tend not to be as hard hit by recession. When money's short, people cut back on BMWs and holidays in Tobago, but they still need clothes and bedlinen and kitchen utensils.' He perches on the edge of his table: 'I don't know what your long-term hopes are, Nina. Did you think, perhaps, of coming back to do bigger campaigns?'

'I hadn't thought in terms of coming back at all, Eric. I've always treated my time here as consultancy work – it just so happens I'm working for friends.' Good one, Sutra!

He smiles. 'You'd be managing our biggest accounts by now – if you'd stayed. As it is, others have filled your shoes. I don't mean that rudely.' He stops while Jane delivers coffees. 'But you still have that flair, Nina. Your team has come up trumps ahead of schedule. Most importantly, they like and trust you.'

I nod, take a sip of over-hot coffee, and burn my mouth.

'What I'm leading up to – I'm sure you've guessed – is that we'd like you to stay. You've done fantastically well in just, what: under seven weeks? If you carry on at this rate, it's possible that in the new year we'll be asking you to take over more specialist projects.'

Buster calls. 'I want to halve my maintenance in the next eighteen months. I have a right to a life.'

I say: 'Buster, we used up your salary every month. And mine. After you went, you gave us only half of it. Now it's reduced to a quarter. *All* my money goes on the house and the kids. I don't have a new car like you. I haven't had three holidays since January, like you. We are only just managing.'

'I'm not *even* managing. Eighteen months, Nina.'

Jack says: 'Mummy, I wish you'd get rich so we didn't just have to *survive.*'

I return home from my weekend away to find the house empty. Laura's sister is about to take a job in Australia. She's invited me for dinner: 'We'll eat at seven forty-five prompt, Nina. They leave for the airport at ten.'

Buster and the children return at seven; an hour after I should have entered the house to find them fed and ready for the bath/bed ritual. He blows up two inflatable hammers they've won at some game, and heads for the front door. He shouts: 'They haven't eaten and I can't stay.'

I shout: 'You'll *have* to do it, Buster. Not only is it part of the access agreement, but I'm getting ready to go out.'

'So am I. I'm late meeting Christine at Belsize Park.'

'Tough. I make twelve out of fourteen evening meals. You do two. *Do* them.'

'How was I to know there'd be a bloody traffic jam?'

'There's a traffic jam every time! Sunday dinner is *your* job, but you've only done it twice in nine months. Tonight, I'm not playing the game, Buster. I'm going to get dressed.'

'Your mother can feed them.'

'She won't be here till half past.'

'Someone's waiting for me in the cold.'

'And someone's waiting for me around a table.'

'They can wait.'

'No they can't. They're catching a flight tonight.' I'm furious that Buster takes it for granted that I'll make the sacrifice. Again.

We hound each other round the kitchen and end up screaming. He bellows: 'You've taken everything I've got. Stop always wanting more!'

I scream: 'I *took* everything? You walked out on it! You walked out on your wife. You walked out on your children. The only thing you can't walk out on is your money! That's the only thing you regret isn't it? YOU BASTARD. You can't even stay and make a meal! Well don't expect me to do it. I'm not your wife any more – I don't cover for you. We're in different camps – I owe you *nothing*.'

Lilla and Jack are at the table. She is colouring busily; blocking us out. He watches; his face turning red with anxiety. Buster storms upstairs to get his things from the spare bedroom. I turn to the kids. I say: 'Listen, this isn't about you. Daddy and I are very stressed. It's not fair that he won't do dinner. It's making me very cross. That's why we're shouting.'

I ring Laura and tell her I won't be coming.

'What's the matter with you, Nina?'

'I'm a bit hysterical. I'll explain in the morning.'

Buster comes back down with his bags. I am filled with loathing. It's a lifetime since I've felt anything but sorrow and, occasionally, contempt, for him. I am surprised at the depth of my anger. He comes in and says something. I turn in a fury: 'Yes: go! GO ON. Why on earth should your obligation to our children take precedence over your obsession with Christine?'

'Don't start this now, Nina!'

'Why not – you selfish self-centred ARSE HOLE.'

He mutters under his breath: 'You fucking bitch,' and leaves the house in a furious door slam.

My mother says: 'Darling, you really must try not to fight in front of the children – it's terribly damaging.'

'How can we not, when the only time we meet is during his access visits?'

I say to Lilla and Jack: 'You know how it is when you're really angry with me? When you're banging doors and shouting and things? What do you say to me?'

'I hate you. I wish you were dead.'

'That's right. And what do you say, Jack?'

'Nothing.'

'That's not true. You always say "You're dead meat, Mummy".' They both laugh. 'Well, it's like that when Daddy and I have a row. What we're really saying is "I hate you and I wish you were dead" – except we say it in a grown-up way; using different words. That's what you've just heard. Right now I hate your Daddy and I really wish he was dead.' I mix olive pesto into the tagliatelle. 'But what happens when *you* calm down, Lilla?'

'We're friends again.'

'That's right. And it's the same with you, isn't it Jack? One minute you're screaming your head off and throwing things, and the next, you want a cuddle.' I dish up. 'Well, that's how it'll be tomorrow when Daddy and I talk on the phone. All the horrible shouting will be forgotten. Do you understand?'

They nod, mouths full of pasta. I laugh and tweak their noses.

Then I march out of the kitchen with my face set like thunder.

Laura sits me down like a recovering invalid: 'We missed you on Sunday, but it wasn't worth getting so angry about.'

'There's a basic principle involved. The only time Buster's responsible for Lilla and Jack is on his weekends – but he can't even manage that. I'm sick of it.'

'It's terribly damaging to fight in front of the children.'

'We're human beings, Laura.'

All those people who berate divorcing couples for involving the children, haven't a clue. If you no longer have a relationship, and the only reason you meet is for the collection or return of progeny, it's inevitable that they'll stand in mute witness to their parents' degeneration. That they'll become the sand bags in the middle of a war zone; absorbing the artillery and sagging under its weight. How could it be otherwise?

I phone Buster's mobile. I'm filled with fury. Nina will look after the kids because . . . Because she does. I want to go outside and scream into the ether, but instead I scream at him and this time he screams back: louder, longer, madly. We tear at each other like ferocious beasts ripping flesh.

Suddenly he bellows: 'It's obvious our bloody marriage never worked. You say we were so happy together – but you've never looked happier than since I went! You're always going out. You're having the time of your *life*.'

Suddenly a calmness comes over me: 'I say Buster, this isn't about our marriage. It's about what's happening now.'

'You should have told me you were going out!'

'It's not *relevant*. I'm supposed to have the children from six o'clock, and they are supposed to be fed.'

Again he's screaming, but I have stopped listening: because I realise this row isn't really about pasta. The money is almost sorted, the access arrangements have long been in place. In just a few weeks, the Decree Absolute will be applied for and granted.

In January of this year we were still, ostensibly, a happily married couple. Successes. By December we will be a sadly divorced couple. Failures.

Knowing what this means, I'm looking forward: defining and redefining the ground rules with which I'll proceed into the future. He is looking back and seeing what he's lost.

And he is angry. Very angry.

Kevin Preston finalises the details: 'So you stay on your current salary for the foreseeable future. It's a healthy amount, but not too much.' He shuts the file. 'Well that clarifies the position. I'll draft the consent and send it to you for approval.'

I lean back in the chair, my hands behind my head: 'We're almost there, aren't we, Kevin?'

'Indeed we are. Almost there. Wasn't that a song by Andy Williams?'

Lawrie and Mala have a second date. He invites her to New York where his American agent is auctioning his book. 'Do you think I should go? It's only five days. Cal and my mum will share the childcare.'

'Of course you should.'

'You don't think it's impetuous and juvenile?'

'Of course I do – but that's more of a reason to do it.'

'No it's not. I think I must be having some sort of mental relapse. It's completely stupid. We've only actually spent seven hours in each other's company.'

'And how many hours on the phone?'

'About twelve.'

'Godsakes, Mala, you're virtually engaged.'

Out of curiousity I pull out my diary and look up the date in January that Buster left us. All it says is 'Lilla's Assembly'. I have drawn some hearts around her name.

I look up the date, three weeks later, that he moved in with Christine. In the afternoon, Maddie and the boys came to tea. In the evening, there's only one entry: 'Snowstorm with Liz. Chelsea Arts Cinema, seven thirty. Mum babysitting.'

Across two pages in July, I have written: children grow up despite their parents.

Only the Decree Nisi gets noted, and even then, just in passing: Decree Nisi through.

So many months of turmoil and turnover. Agony and ecstasy. Where are they in my record of life?

I turn on the radio. Leann Rimes: how do I live without you.

People say: 'You've done so well, Nina. You've bounced back where others would fall by the wayside.'

I just grin, because I know the truth.

I am still at the wayside: but I know the road on which I've found myself will lead to better things.

Mala pulls me up with a naughty grin: 'All it needs is violins.' I roll my eyes. We leave the Harrods shrine to Diana and Dodi and head for the ice-cream fountain. 'What does it mean, Egyptian escalators? You half expect them to be covered in hieroglyphics.' She shoves a dairy wish-list in my direction: 'So things are getting awkward with the ex?'

'It's a little bit scary. For both of us, I think.'

'You'll come out best, Nina. Freedom isn't leaving your wife for another woman: that's serial slavery.'

We order chocolate milkshakes. Mala says: 'Is taking lace pyjamas to New York a bit too "fuck me"?'

'They would be for the cinema, but given that you and Lawrie are sharing a bedroom, I don't see that it matters.'

'I suppose not.' She giggles. 'It's crazy isn't it?'

'Just don't marry him, that's all.'

'I'm not in the market for marriage.' She chases the last bits of froth in her glass with a straw: 'My mother accused me of being like Bethany – my road protestor friend. You know, the one with four kids by different men.'

'Because you're going to Houston?'

'Because I'm going with a *man*. I'm becoming a loose woman, apparently.' We both crack up. Mala says: 'I'm about to take over as deputy editor of a national newspaper.

I've got three wonderful children and a beautiful house that I pay for myself; but my mum's worrying that I'm not virginal. Weird, isn't it?'

'I'm so proud of you, Darling.'
'Why?'
'You're so positive, so bright: you've taken the sting out of Buster's departure for all of us. Even the children are starting to thrive. Lilla just showed me her workbook. No more strange pictures – she's writing again. It's a hell of an achievement.'
'You've got to say that, Mum, because you love me.'
'I'd love you even if you were falling apart.' She shakes her head: 'I don't know what your sister would have done in the same situation. You know what Maddie's like – even as a baby she loved her routines. The minute something goes out of kilter she practically has a nervous breakdown.'
I look at her carefully, wondering if she's had wind of Maddie's disquiet; but there's no sign. I watch, holding Jack in my lap, as she runs the nit comb through Lilla's hair again and again. I say: 'Maddie and Gavin will be together for ever.'
'Oh I think so. They're well matched. Salt and pepper.'
'That's what you used to say about me and Buster.'
'It's what I still say about you and Buster.'
I hug my son to me and bury my nose, as ever, in the soft part at the back of his neck: this boy who moves like a boxer; who moves like his Daddy. I say: 'It's true, isn't it? We were salt and pepper. It just goes to show there's no logic to life.'

Will Davis believes that truth comes to us in flashes.
I say: 'Like taking off your Wonderbra and realising that at the end of the day, a pair of saggy boobs is a pair of saggy boobs?'
'I wouldn't know about that. But sometimes, you can be driving along and suddenly have a flash of insight.'

'Give me a for-instance.'

'For instance, the week before I married Flora, I was in the bath when I suddenly thought: 'I don't love her. I *do not* love her.'

'You've never said that before.'

'Because, by the next morning, I'd decided that I was wrong.' I roll my eyes. He says: 'The point is, Nina: I was right. Within a year the whole thing had disintegrated.'

'And that turns your moment of bathtime misgiving into a revelatory experience?'

'It was a flash of truth.'

'Surely no truer than your deciding the next morning that you *did* love her. You can find meaning in anything if you choose to, Will. I was really content with Buster, but I'm also incredibly happy without him: does that mean we should never have married? Of course not. It just shows that each of us has the capacity to live different types of life with a degree of success.'

Over a working lunch with Samir and Cathy we talk about reinventing products: how changing the depth of a gusset can turn a pair of slinky mini-briefs into practical but sexy day wear. Cathy giggles into what looks like a plate of whale spume: 'You've been doing that the other way round, Nina.'

Samir winks at me. 'You were always good at wool-pulling.'

'I'm bloody brilliant at it now. You should see what I've achieved at home. I've shoved a whole new morality into place.'

'Meaning?'

'I tell the kids that what their father's done is not bad/neglectful/cruel/selfish/thoughtless – it just happens in life that grown-ups fall out of love and sometimes remove themselves without working through either a period of attempted restructuring or resignation.'

'And?'

'Therefore, I tell them, this does not mean that you will suffer from a reduction in the time/affection/attention/money your father lavished on you – merely that it will be redistributed in a more random manner. Life will not change with just one parent to bring up the slack, because Mummy loves you and she will never leave you. She may be more stressed/ tired/angry/distracted/ depressed than previously – but you'll hardly notice.'

Cathy looks embarrassed. Samir nods slowly. 'I get it.'

'And now you wish you'd never asked.'

Buster arrives with a smile on his face: 'I'm going to rejig the next few weekends. We're going away.'

'Again?'

He snorts: 'You don't understand the strain that Christine and I are suffering – nothing to do with *our* relationship: it's all external factors – of which you're one, Nina.'

I shake my head in disbelief. In the background Go West are on VH1. 'The King of Wishful Thinking'. Buster says: 'Thank God I left you: it's clear you have no perspective on my needs.'

'Mummy, Daddy says you're taking all his money.'

'Really? And what does he say I'm *taking* it for?'

'He says he's got nothing because of you.'

'Lilla, why do you think Daddy *gives* me the money? Is it to have my toenails painted by ladies in nylon coats, or is it because that's what pays for the house and for you?'

'Because of the house?'

'Right. And who's always paid for the house and for you, Lilla?'

'Daddy?'

'Yes, Daddy. Now that Daddy's gone, he's only paying for *some* of the house and *some* of you. I pay the rest. One day

I'll pay most of it. So, the next time your Daddy complains about money, ask if he'd like you to starve. Okay?'

'An exciting weekend ahead?'
   'Hopefully.'
   'I won't wait up then.'
   I follow Gavin as he carries my bag to the spare room. I say: 'I don't think I've ever told you how important you are in my life. In *all* our lives. You're a terrific man, Gavin. Maddie's very lucky.'
   'Would you mind telling her that?'
   'I think she already knows.'
   He looks awkward. 'She's a bit preoccupied at the moment. They start the actual filming next week. I hadn't realised how time-consuming television is. Even when she's home, the phone goes every ten minutes.' He sighs; I smile; and suddenly he comes across and gives me a hug: 'Let's make this a mutual admiration society. You've been a real star, Nina. People can be destroyed by marriage break-ups but you're always looking on the bright side. It's terrific.'
   I look at him suspiciously: 'Is this a conspiracy? First Mum gives me a little speech; now it's you. Does this mean that in reality you're worried about me?'
   'No, it's genuine. As Maddie said only this morning: if you make it seem any easier, we'll all be splitting up.'

As the months have passed, everyone seems surprised that I've made the best of things. As if there's a choice in these matters. As if there's room for self-pity and mourning.
   When of course, there isn't.

Will calls. 'I've got a friend I'd like you to meet. Are you free this weekend?'
   'Tonight I'm seeing Mala and the girls: she's off to Houston on Monday. Tomorrow daytime, I'm helping

Laura make costumes for the school concert, but I'm free in the evening.'

'I'll arrange something for around eight.'

We meet for drinks off Ladbroke Grove, at The Cobden. Mala's found us sofas. I say: 'I think I should have a divorce party – with a ceremony and stuff. A sort of unmarriage. My uncle could walk me back down the aisle and hand me over to my mum.'

'We could make an effigy of Buster and bury it in your garden.'

'I'd wear scarlet – and the black veil from turkey night.'

'You could arrive in a coach and four.'

'Not a coach and four, Caroline. I don't want to look like the Queen. I'll see if someone at the agency has a Merc or something.'

Mala says: 'I think it's a brilliant idea to celebrate. We make such a fuss about getting married, you need to lay it to rest with a ceremony too. Would there be a priest?'

'Not a real one!'

'It might make a good feature. It'd help with costs.'

'I'm not looking for newspaper coverage.'

'Shame.' She passes round the bowl of nuts and watches with interest as I grab a handful and crunch them up. 'We recently ran a piece about the scientific analysis of a bowl of bar nuts. They found traces of thirty-one different strains of male urine. Makes you think, doesn't it?'

Laura's children are building a tent in the sitting room: two duvets, four pillows, eight cushions, three chairs, an ottoman, a tricycle, two dishcloths and the mophead. I wonder what Lilla and Jack are doing and feel a deep pang of longing. Laura drags me into the kitchen where old sheets are being turned into togas.

'Any news?'

I start hemming neckholes. 'Not really. We're still scream-ing over money, but that's to be expected.'

'Very civilised.' Threading the sewing machine she mutters: 'I notice you don't mention love any more.'

'Love doesn't have any relevance.'

'If Alan left me, I couldn't stop loving him so easily.'

'That's what I used to say about Buster, but the truth is, you don't know how you'll react until it happens.'

'I'd be so hurt and bitter.'

'You don't have to be.' I stop for a moment, lost in thought. Happy-sad thoughts. 'I loved Buster so much, Laura. He was soft and funny and fun. But he was also a grown-up with a vast brain. I loved his integrity; his mind: that was such a large part of him. When he went, all the values he represented, died. I was ashamed of him; disappointed. He *wasn't* the man I'd married. Does that make sense?' She nods uncertainly. 'It's like that Steps song and now you're suddenly like a stranger.' She laughs. I say: 'I don't *know* Buster.'

'Maybe you *have* to tell yourself that. To let go.'

'If that's the case, thank God I'm gullible enough to believe it.'

Mala says: 'Don't mention New York to Josh, Caroline.'

'I thought my brother was only a friend.'

'That's exactly why.' Mala looks impish. 'Now what about the two of you? What's your view on ads, Caroline?'

'I'm afraid I'm not that desperate.'

'Wrong.' With the smugness of a woman who's been seeing the same man for more than a week, she pulls the *Guardian* Guide out of her bag. Flicking through the listings she stops at the personals: 'Men Seeking Women. Let's see if there's anything of interest.'

Across the room, two glass-eyed blokes, high on cocaine, sit in companionable silence with their blank women friends. The blonde is a well-known aristocrat; the black girl a celebrated rock chick. Jeeze, I think, if that's the best *they* can do, what hope is there for the rest of us?

Mala reads. 'Troilus seeks Cressida. Hmmm. Well undressed man requires Barbie with easy-remove wardrobe. Sensitive, tactile, honest and kind: Cancerian designer wants long-haired pussycat to stroke. Please!' She cocks a finger. 'Here's one for you, Nina: socialist anarchist nuclear physicist, needs woman with atom of sense for fusion experiments.'

'I only do cold fusion, Mala.'

'This is it! Two psychologists, early thirties, seek lively women for food, fun, flicks and flirting. I'm going to ring them.'

Caroline is lost in thought. I point to a table of young men in the restaurant area: 'Straight or gay?'

'I can't tell the difference any more.'

Mala is calling someone on her mobile phone. Slowly, I realise she is punching in the digits of the voicemail box number. With her finger to her lip she listens and smiles.

Mala says: 'Hello. My name's Nina. I'm in my thirties, I work in advertising, and I'm very presentable. Well, you don't need to put a paperbag over my head.' She pauses. 'Not after twilight, anyway.' She grins as we both look up. 'I'm solvent and I'm single and I'm lots of fun. Like you, I'm looking as much for company as romance. My friend's called Caroline. She's fresh in from the wilderness and needs some excitement in her life.'

Caroline, outraged, barks: 'Who are you talking to, Mala?' And then, as the penny drops: 'How dare you!'

'And if you fancy taking a little gamble, we'd love to meet up with you.' Mala gives my direct-line number slowly; clearly. 'I'm there during the day so why not call and we can get together?'

Will says: 'This is Ben – we were at school together. He's

been in Exeter the past three years, but he's just got a consultant's job in London.'

'What do you do, Ben?'

'I'm a gynaecologist.' I look across to Will. He grins and nods. I shake my head disbelievingly. Ben says accusingly: 'What's wrong with being a gynaecologist?'

'I don't know.' And really I don't; but somehow the thought of being set up with a man who inspects women's innards for a living is deeply off-putting. I think about my occasional stress incontinence. My PMT. My two long labours. My listing pelvic floor. The perineal stretching. Tampons; speculums, Dutch caps; eggs. I look at him and am lost for words.

By ten, we're back at Will's place in Bloomsbury because, having not eaten for forty-eight hours – 'I've been too busy' – he gets rat-arsed and tired. Once there, he falls asleep on the sofa. Ben says: 'He's out for the count. Look, I'm staying ten minutes away at the Marriott – shall we head there and get a sandwich or something?'

We get the sandwiches on room service because there's a good in-house movie and a definite spark. So he's a gynaecologist: what the hell. As time goes on, I'm aware that it's too soon for anything serious; so why be picky about encounters?

I sit in one of the chairs while Ben sprawls on the bed. As the food arrives he pats the space next to him: 'Kick your shoes off and climb on – I promise not to pounce unless you look willing.'

I do as instructed. I say: 'What does willing look like?'

He stares at me and I smile. He pulls me to him. 'It looks just like that.'

Still Jack asks: 'Why doesn't Daddy live here any more?'

'You know why, Darling. Because he lives with Christine.'

'Why does he live with Christine?'

'Because he loves her.'

'Why doesn't he love us?'

'He does. He just doesn't live here, that's all.'

'When you unmarry Daddy, will you get a new husband?'

'I don't need a new husband right now, Little One. I have you and Lilla. That's more than enough to make me happy.'

Afterwards, Ben and I lie in the half dark, our legs entwined around each other. We talk a little about Will, and a lot about Ben. He tells me his hopes and dreams, his achievements and ambitions. I listen with half an ear, making the right noises and thinking about love.

Love making: harmless, ungainly, silly. The most potent weapon that men and women can use against each other. I wonder: if I ever fell in love again, would I feel sexually anxious? Would I worry about fidelity? What have I learned from my complete lack of interest in Buster's external sexuality?

Perhaps genuine sexual jealousy is confined to the first throes of passion: that time when our partners are still enigmas to us. Unpossessed souls with secrets yet uncovered. Or is it always there: a measure of our love? Certainly, up until the moment Buster told me of Christine, I believed I was consumed by it. Then, within seconds, sex seemed so insignificant in the great scheme of things. So meaningless.

Ben says: 'Do you mind if I have a Joe?'

'A Joe?'

'A cigarette. A smoky Joe.'

'No. Of course not.'

He gets up and pads across the room to his jacket. 'I'm down to five a day. I just find them so relaxing after . . . activity.'

I lie there looking at him in his fleshy white nakedness.

Not a bad-looking man. Nice love handles. Pert bum. In far better nick than me. Not that I care. Because of course, sleeping with a gynaecologist has its compensations. One: he's dealt with every permutation of the female form, so there are no surprises. Two: he can identify and locate a clitoris without a roadmap and magnifying glass.

He comes back to the bed, picks the eiderdown off the floor and puts it over us. 'We still haven't eaten our sandwiches.'

'I'm not hungry.'

'You must eat something. Otherwise you won't have the energy to do it all again.'

'Are you trying to tell me something?'

He stubs out the fag and stuffs a ham and tomato sarnie in his mouth. 'I should have warned you. I'm a man with a big appetite.'

Anne-Marie approaches as I push the incline level up to ten on the treadmill. Sweat is pouring off me because I haven't seen the gym in four weeks. She leans across, watching. 'Long time no see, Nina.' She says it loud so I hear her above the sound in my headphones: Lighthouse Family, 'Lifted'. I've declined Maddie's roast goose lunch for this. I ignore her. 'You ought to come to my GAQ attack classes – get that abdomen tightened. I've had one woman go from Hattie Jacques to Dannie Behr in a month.' I nod. 'You're nice-looking, Nina. We should do a before and after.'

'This *is* after.'

'Other mothers beg me to help them get their figures back. They hate having sagging bums and loose stomachs. Have you tried Weight Watchers?'

'Anne-Marie, most days I only get one meal. It's quite hard to fit in lunch when you're working your bollocks off.'

'Eating late at night, Nina. That's what does it. Every mouthful consumed after seven, turns into fat – did you know that?'

In the early hours I gather my bits and pieces and head for the door. Ben mumbles 'Where are you going?'

'Home. I don't want my sister to find me missing.'

'You're an adult.'

'I'm an adult having a one-night stand. I'd rather keep it to myself, if that's all right with you.'

'Human beings need sex. It's life affirming.'

'I agree with you; but she unfortunately doesn't.'

He shakes his head. 'Write your number for me somewhere.'

'You're not going to call, Ben. Let's just leave it.'

'Have I done something wrong? Didn't I satisfy you?'

'It's not that—'

'Then what is it?'

'I don't want to play games. Like most men, you just want my number to show you can get it. That you've made the kill. Let's be honest: this is just an encounter. It's suited us both. Who are we pretending for?'

I wake up with my nether regions aflame: I've got thrush.

Why is such a hideous disorder named after a songbird? It should be called crow or chicken. Or cuckoo, because you don't want it in your nest, but somehow it's planted itself there.

Cathy says: 'Too much sex, Nina.'

'One night!'

'Divine judgement for all that friction.'

I think back forty-eight hours; to that night of madness; badness. The way he made me talk while he was inside, so he could keep going indefinitely. Sometimes stopped altogether. I sigh: what a shame about his personality.

'You didn't use a condom, did you?'

'Thrush isn't a sexually transmitted disease, Cathy. I'd still have got it even if we had used condoms.'

'Men can carry it though.' She drops her voice: 'You ought to know better. He may have something much *worse*.'

'Given he's a gynaecologist, it's hardly likely.' But inside, I'm discomfited by my own lack of care.

Cathy saunters to the doorway and then shouts across the office: 'You can't assume he's clap free because he's a gynaecologist, Nina. All it means is he gets the antibiotics quicker.'

'Nina – have you got a moment?'

Eric Casey smiles as I enter his office: 'You look suspicious.'

'I sense bad news.'

'You're clearly the Mystic Meg of BCAF.' He motions to a chair but I remain standing. 'You've heard the rumours. We're putting a few things on ice.' I nod. 'That includes the expansion of Bugle Direct for the forseeable future.'

'How far ahead is forseeable?'

'It could be three weeks, three months or three years. What I'm saying is the spirit is still willing but, momentarily, the body is weak. We need to watch the world markets – any threat of recession affects our flotation.' He looks at me carefully; kindly: 'It's a temporary freezing of everything. Even wages. Is that all right?'

'The freezing of wages is never all right, Eric.'

As the Absolute looms, Buster becomes like a cornered beast. Each little clause, agreed together in civilised moments, suddenly comes under renewed scrutiny. He makes threats, withdraws promises, questions the validity of his own wording. I find myself screaming at him, angry and confused by his last-minute brinkmanship. His response is increased intransigence. I say: 'Buster, I will only talk to you through my solicitor.'

Caroline is horror struck: 'I told Mala, now I'm telling you. Following up personal ads is is not my idea of amusement.'

'It's just one hour of your time. All Bar One, Oxford Circus, at eight.' I ignore her complaints. 'It's a laugh, Caroline. They sound fun. They're called Ed and James. One does isometric testing for a recruitment company, the other's in personnel.'

'We don't all enjoy exploring the unknown, Nina.'

'Perhaps we should?'

'Put that down in proposal form and I'll consider it.'

It's a throw-away line, but Caroline has set me thinking. I start making notes in pads and on scraps of paper around the house. A sort of Nina Sutra guide to picking yourself up off the floor and focusing forwards, no matter what. A guide to fashioning your own destiny and pulling your children up with you.

Why should the shadows of our past dominate our lives, when it's the future, and how we approach it, that matters? I stick a sign on my word processor: It's time wives started to party.

'Actually, you're the sixth pair we've met in five days.'

'Goodness, you have been busy.' Caroline eyes me malevolently over a glass of white wine.

'We wouldn't tell you that if you weren't a vast improvement on the sort of women we've been coming up against.'

'And what sort of women are those?'

They start laughing, sharing a private joke. 'Well, the first pair were nurses. They met us in a champagne bar and didn't pay for a single drink.' Caroline sneers. 'Then there were two primary school teachers who never said a word.'

'But they were nice-looking girls, weren't they, Ed?'

'Oh yeah. Very nice. Just completely silent. I tried sign language on them, but it didn't even raise a smile.'

James says: 'That's because he signed "fuck off".' They roar with laughter: 'Just a joke, girls.'

Ed swigs from his bottle of Becks. 'Who was the third date – the students or the Shell women?'

'Shell.' James winces. 'One was a geologist and the other – I can't remember. Look girls, I'm not being rude here, but you couldn't have sold them to a zoo, they were so ugly.'

The two of them are semi-hysterical. I start to laugh, too; because it's so absurd. Caroline is unmoving; unmoved. Ed says: 'The last pair, we met just before you, actually. In the Cheers bar at five thirty. That's why we're a bit pissed. We'd written them off as uninteresting, but they weren't all bad.'

'What did *they* do?'

'Computers. The Millennium Bug. They advise on blips.'

Caroline leans across the table and hisses: 'I wonder if they could advise us on escaping *this* particular blip?'

'Mum, can you babysit next Saturday? I'm going to an awards dinner with Paul from the office.'

'Of course, Darling. What are you going to wear?'

'I don't know. Something black.'

'Why not buy yourself a new dress. You deserve it.'

Afterwards Caroline and I walk across to Mash in Great Portland Street. 'I've just made a killing on a rat-infested Docklands warehouse. It's my shout.'

For the first few minutes we say nothing, leaning back and watching the punters around the big hop mashing machines. We go to the loo to inspect the well reported sink arrangement: a hole in the wall. Finally she says: 'It wasn't as bad as I'd imagined.'

'They were interesting and passably intelligent.'

'But it's not a passport to love is it, Nina?' She pulls out a YSL cigarette and taps it on the table. 'Why don't you sit back and let love find you – assuming that's what you want.'

My mother says: 'I still love Buster, you know. He's been a fool, but he's essentially honourable. I just don't know how he did what he did.'

'It's one of life's great imponderables. Hanif Kureishi says men do it because they can.'

'Because they can?'

'Yes. Because, I suppose, they know that the women will always pick up the pieces. They'll brush themselves down, put the kids first, and somehow work their way past it.'

In the doctor's waiting room, I meet a local mum. 'Hello, stranger. I miss our playground gossips now you're back at work. Is everything all right? Are you keeping the house?' I smile and nod. She says: 'No wonder you're looking so well.'

Inside the surgery I run through the symptoms of a problem that has started recurring with unpleasant frequency. The doctor examines me. 'It looks like you're suffering biliary colic. It fits in with what you're describing – a cross between a heart attack and giving birth. I'm afraid, of course, it's aggravated by stress.' She runs up a prescription: 'Anti-inflammatories, fairly standard pain killers and some extra-strong antacids. If you get another attack lasting more than a couple of hours, call the emergency locum for a shot of pethidine.' She sees my face. 'I'm sorry, but that's the best I can do.'

*   *   *

The shop in Brent Cross is full of overblown evening dresses: the sort of thing you'd wear if you were twenty and looked like a pipe cleaner. A pipe cleaner with blown-up silicone titties, that is. I work my way through the racks despondently. Nothing in John Lewis; nothing in Fenwick; nothing in any of the small boutiques; and just half an hour before the centre shuts.

An over made-up older woman in a tight black skirt suit, sidles up to me: 'Are you looking for a particular style or colour, Madam?'

'I need something understated for a grand evening event.'

'Do you want to display, or simply intimate?' I look at her blankly. She makes a figure of eight with her hands. 'What's the intention: to promise or to tease?' I look down at my uncertain protruberances, uncertainly.

Her face suddenly softens. 'Leave it to me.'

'Mummy, do you want to see my letter to Father Christmas?'

'It's a bit early for that, Lilla.'

'It's only six weeks and two days.'

Is it? 'That's still quite a long time.'

'Will Daddy be coming?'

'We can ask him.'

'Then he'll come.'

'He may not, Sweetheart.'

'Both my grannies have said they'll come.'

'Then it won't matter so much if Daddy doesn't. Will it?'

I put on the dress and bless the woman in the shop. It transforms me. The V of the neck is loose cut and then clinched tightly at the waist, taking me in and out at the right places. The fact that it's slightly off shoulder means the tops of my arms are covered, and the turquoise green sets off my hazel eyes. The sheathed lower half tapers neatly at my ankles.

For the first time in years, I pull out the expensive paste

necklace and studs I bought for my wedding, but never wore. *Faux* diamonds and emeralds – to set off the ring I no longer wear.

The overall effect, even with dirty hair kirby-gripped upwards, is really quite exciting. I twirl in front of the mirror and admire myself. I think: this is the first time in years I've dressed up for someone who isn't my husband. Dating Nick and flirting with Tag, the look was decidedly street chic. This is something different altogether. Womanly.

I close my eyes and imagine myself dancing with Paul; being held in solid, trusted, arms. Resting my head on a broad, older, masculine, shoulder. The kids are in bed; there's no one about. I go down and put on Ella Fitzgerald: 'Let's Fall In Love'. And I dance with my invisible suitor.

'Maddie, have you thought about Christmas?'

'Of course. You'll be coming to us, won't you?'

'I don't know. Maybe I should maintain the usual routine?'

'It'll be a bit lonely, Nina.'

'I thought, perhaps, you could all come to us.'

'But Buster's always done your cooking. I remember last year's bread sauce. Delia; not as good as mine. The kitchen was in chaos and the two of you were barely speaking.' She notes my silence down the phone. 'Well we didn't know what he was up to then, did we? We all thought it was work.' She sighs: 'Look, it's very sweet of you, Nina, and I know this first Christmas is important – but I'm such a pedant when it comes to food and you can barely do a basic bolognese sauce.'

I smile sweetly at the wall: 'Well, to be honest Maddie, what I thought was that we'd have Christmas at *my* house – but you'd do all the actual cooking, and the rest of us would wash up.'

*   *   *

Paul stands at the door, just looking. I suddenly want him so much, it's all I can do not to pull him through. To imprison him, alone. Except of course, the sounds of Lilla and Jack fighting with my mother are wafting down the stairs. The screws in this prison, are still loose.

Finally he says: 'You're beautiful,' and motions me out.

In the car, we barely speak.

At the ball, he heads the receiving line. For a while I stand dutifully, decoratively, at his side, but I'm restless. He whispers: 'I had no idea I had to do this. If you want to wander off, I'll extricate myself at the first opportunity and find you.'

The bar is awash with familiar faces. Eric Casey and his wife beckon me across. She and I discuss children while he schmoozes a posse from the ITC. 'I hate these dos, don't you?' she asks. 'Nothing but industry gossip.'

'That's precisely why I love them.'

'Of course. You would.' Innocently: 'You're here with Paul?'

'He didn't have a partner for the night.'

'He's a lovely man; needs someone to take him out of himself.' She studies me for a reaction.

I smile. Innocently. Suddenly he's at my side. 'I couldn't stand it any longer. Shall we find somewhere a little less claustrophobic?' He guides me back outside, past the later arrivals, and we turn the corner at a large black-glassed building that marks Curzon Street.

I say: 'Can you remember when this was the Playboy Club? When I was little, we'd stand on Park Lane and watch the silhouettes through the windows: bunnies with drink trays and men with cigars pacing at gaming tables.'

'I didn't grow up in London.' He's tense. He says: 'We've got half an hour. The meal isn't till eight thirty.'

We wander down as far as Shepherd's Market, stopping

in the arched entrance, yards from the old Manticore office and RCA Records. It's chilly. I say: 'Are you all right, Paul?'

'I'm anxious. You make me anxious.' He looks embarrassed. 'God, Nina, you look so . . . I was really hoping tonight . . .' He shakes his head. 'What sort of an idiot would leave you?'

His eyes are impenetrable in the neon glow. I want to push back his thinning dark thatch and trace the furrow between his brows. I want to touch his face and feel the hint of dark stubble on his jaw. To follow the shape of his wide, gentle, mouth with my fingers. Suddenly, he puts out his hand and brushes a tendril of hair off my cheek. Instinctively I turn and brush it with my lips. We stare at each other, both uncertain what to do. Somewhere a clock chimes the quarter. He looks at his watch and sighs, offering me his arm: 'Come on or we'll miss the meal.'

Why does love never happen the way you want it to? The night you're jammed into your sexiest underwear is the night you get stood up by your date. The moment when you're ready to give all to a man you barely know, a meal beckons.

Life is full of lost moments and unrequited longing.

When I was eighteen we'd go to clubs feeling hot, high and ready for love – and the only blokes who'd ask us to dance were either half-cut or four inches too short. So many opportunities lost for . . . lack of opportunity.

As Paul and I walked back to the grand ballroom, I thought back to moments in my life when I almost had something – someone – in my grasp, and then mislaid them. Boyfriends scattered across the wilderness of my memory like safari animals glimpsed through binoculars.

Matthew Mark Luke John: I could have had all four gospels.

Paul, John, George, Ringo: and three Beatles' name-sakes.
Bing, Bob, Dean and Sammy: two of the ancient crooners.
Philip, Charles, Andrew, Edward: at least one of the Royals.
Jarvis, Liam, Noel: No, none of those.
So many men with whom I never made second base.

'Buster, you know you're welcome to come here for Christmas.' I sense his fear. 'Lunch or dinner: we can tailor it to suit you.'
'I'm not really sure what we're doing.'
'It's just that you've always been here, you know. Mornings when the children bring in their stockings; afternoons for lunch and the social thing; evenings doing tree presents and playing charades—'
'The only reason we did all that, was because you insisted, Nina. I hate the commercialism. It's *you* who wants trees and parties and all that nonsense. You don't need me to make it work for you.'
'You don't make anything work for me any more, Buster. I'm thinking about the children. Don't eat; just pop by for an hour.'
He flusters around, angrily. 'I don't know what we're doing for Christmas. It's so bloody unimportant.'
'If it's that unimportant, Christine surely won't mind if you spend a little time with your children.'

The speeches are unexpectedly short and amusing. There are only twelve prizes to be awarded for the major campaign successes of the year. As Chair of the ALMC, Paul rattles through the presentations at speed while, simultaneously, giving the impression that his role is effortless and considered. I sit watching with a glass of wine in my hand; enchanted by him.

At one point Axel rustles past: 'How's it going with Romeo? A number of people have said how good you look together.'

'I don't need this right now.'

'You don't need the gossip or you don't need Paul Avedon?'

'I don't need either.'

He kisses me loudly on the forehead: 'You're so sweet, Nina.'

Very occasionally, Paul looks in my direction; his eyes give nothing away. Somehow I find this ten times more exciting than the smouldering uncertainty we shared outside. It's so cold, so hard: so bastardly professional.

Why do women like bastards? What is it about uninterested, unfeeling men that increases the pulse?

'I think it's that bastards bring out our sexuality: because that's the only way we can win them over. They make us feel like real women: not mothers, not wives, not providers, not facilitators, but predatory, earthy, excited and whole.'

'That sounds like something you'd read on an advertising hoarding.' Liz laughs: 'They're all the same, Nina.'

'No: a bastard isn't needy. He's not after feeding or fussing or settling or sex. He's self-contained – and that makes *us* desperate for his approval, and *him* enormously powerful.'

'We don't have to fall for it.'

'But we do, don't we? Because we want to be wanted. If we can't pull it off with our skills, that only leaves our sexuality.'

'Because most men can be won over through their pricks?'

'It's the universal avenue of approach.' We laugh.

Bastards free our spirits and enable us to live out our fantasies. They allow us to express areas of our nature that may otherwise be sidelined as base or unwomanly. They also have a habit of breaking our hearts: but that's a small price to pay for the fun, isn't it?

I gaze at a point somewhere stage left, so that if and when Paul looks at me, my attention is elegantly engaged elsewhere. I surreptitiously drop one of my dress straps, so it's almost off the shoulder. And then I get lost in thought, remembering my first days at BCAF; God, I was so excited by it all.

Paul's then wife, Lois Flaherty, would laugh as I appeared in her office with yet another storyboard for something or other: 'Nina – just sit down for five minutes and come up with one definitive line. You've run four possible themes by me – all of them with potential. Now decide which best conveys what we're trying to say, and why. Then come back.'

Crazy Lois who fell in love over one wild weekend with an Italian car designer – and fled to New York when it destroyed her marriage. Lovely, lissome Lois and her perfect partner, Paul.

I wonder whether, if they'd been together ten years and had two children, she would have acted so rashly; or if Paul would have been so unforgiving. Somehow I think not. Having children eclipses everything else: particularly something as trivial as infatuation. Infatuation, surely, is the spark that fires instant passion? I wonder to myself if I am thinking now of Lois or Buster. Buster who, so clearly and passionately, loves himself above all others; or Lois, who lost herself to lust.

Suddenly Paul is there beside me. 'Come on – I've promised to get things started.' He takes my hand and leads me to the floor. Robbie Williams: 'Angels'. He pulls me close, his arm around my waist: 'Let's do it the old-fashioned way; it gives me an excuse to hold you.'

*   *   *

Mala is squirming on her sofa. I say warily: 'Please don't tell me you've become the sixth woman to accept a proposal from Lawrie Grimes.' She rolls her eyes. 'Or the eighth to live with him?' She shakes her head crossly. I grin: 'Why do you keep fidgeting, Mala? You're like a circus flea.'

'He can't get an erection without cocaine.'

'Does he sprinkle it on the end like Parmesan?'

'Very funny. I spent the whole time in fear of being busted.'

'So it's over?'

'I'm not sure. He's brilliant fun. Honestly Nina, I could sit and talk with him for ever. He's more eclectic than Jay and more creative than Cal. It was a bit like you with Buster – we just locked into each other. He's full of ideas.'

'Can he be retrained to take Viagra?'

She sighs: 'Do they sell it in powder form?'

Back in his car, Paul says: 'Thanks for being such a beautiful and dutiful date. Next time I'll try and find something a little less stressful to tempt you with.'

'I enjoyed myself.'

'Did you? I have an aversion to industry back-slapping.'

'I must have missed all that during an alcoholic episode.'

He turns into Park Lane and heads north towards the Edgware Road. Again he is silent. I don't know what to say. I sense all chances of romance slipping slowly from my grasp. He clearly likes me; I feel certain he fancies me; but there's a barrier there – something that's stopping him taking the next step. I recognise it, but I don't understand it.

Suddenly he says: 'Did you ever find Mr Wrong?'

'No, I'm still looking. D'you know any potential takers?' He ignores the opening as we pull up outside my house. He sees me to the door. I pull my wrap around me: 'It would be nice to have *some* sort of relationship, but most of my energy goes into the children and work. It'd be a very special man who didn't take umbrage at being so far down my list of priorities.'

Kissing me chastely, he says: 'If he was a special man, he might be granted equal status.'

'Even *equal* status is difficult for a lot of men to swallow.'

Right up until Jack was born Buster would ask: 'Who do you love more, me or Lilla?' and I would always answer: 'I love you the same, but differently. I love you because I chose you; and I love her because we made her and she's ours.' After Jack, I tried answering in the same vein, but it wasn't true. And so I changed my response: 'I love you more than I ever have, Buster; but I love the children in a more intense way.'

'What do you mean, intense?'

'They're so small and innocent and needy; their worlds revolve around me and mine around them. Whatever they do, I'll love them. But you, you have your own life and your own interests; you're independent. That affects the nature of love.'

'So you love me less?'

'No! I love you more than I ever have. Much more, even, than when we married. But if love is a measure of who you'd save first from a burning building – then I would save them. Does that answer the question?'

'Mummy, can I wear this necklace?'

'No, Sweetheart; it's too precious.'

'Where's it from?'

'Well I bought it a long time ago – to wear on my wedding day – but it clashed with my flowers so I put it away – until last night when I went to a very grand dance.'

'And that man came to take you.'

'That's right.'

'I liked that man.'

'You didn't even see him, Lilla.'

'I saw him from my window. He looked nice.'

'Did he?' I stroke my daughter's head gently. With the Absolute so close, she's starting to panic. She knows her father will still be there, yet she doesn't trust him. She wants a substitute: just in case. The anxiety that I sensed in the summer is unabated; every male visitor is a potential replacement.

Even one that never got further than the door.

Mala says: 'I've told Lawrie I won't see him unless he leaves his drugs at home. The last thing I need is to feature on my own front page as the girlfriend of a drug-taking crime writer. Some risks just aren't worth it.' Our children come rushing through the room. She shoos them out with promises of Jaffa Cakes. 'I only got back in the early hours of this morning. I'm exhausted.'

I say: 'Don't play with fire, Mala.'

'The only fires in my life, Nina, are old flames.'

Later, we meet with Laura's brood in the park. Her youngest has a balloon tied to his wrist; the other two have bikes which are immediately abandoned. As they run off together, screaming, we sit on a bench enjoying the last embers of autumn sun.

Laura says: 'Alan's jacking in his job.'

'What for?'

'Glass ceiling time. Too many others waiting to jump into the dead man's shoes. We talked it through and decided he could either stick it out, get steadily frustrated and take it out on us at home; or he could try going it alone.'

'That's very grown-up of you.'

'I didn't want a replay of what happened to you, Nina. A

man's ambition causes so much strain doesn't it? Whenever we went out with you and Buster, it was non-stop court and chambers. When Alan starts on finance, I switch off.'

'That was Buster's biggest accusation against *me*: that I'd started switching off. His job is his life.'

'Alan and I did so much talking after Buster went. Everyone did, I suppose. There but for the grace of God go I.' She stops and points upwards at the helium parrot that has left her child's arm and is floating fast away in the ether. 'We both feel that what we've got is so precious, we must protect it.'

'I envy you, Laura.'

'And sometimes I envy you, Nina. For all the attendant problems, it seems to me you're having the time of your life.'

I say: 'Listen, Laura. I've probably said this a hundred times, but given a choice, I'd rather have stayed married. I'm a big big girl in a big big world, but the children have suffered. I still believe in marriage; in seeing the bad times through.'

'Better not to risk bad times, though.'

'Very few of us are clever enough to see them coming.'

In my lunch hour I draft and redraft lists on my word processor.

Friends to be invited to the divorce party.

Special roles to be allocated as part of the fun.

Items to be begged and borrowed: clothing, cars, decorations, dog collars, head-dresses, bunting; a tent.

Different types of finger food matched against the number of available ovens within five minutes walk of our house.

Endless dithering over what sort of drinks people should bring.

A changing soundtrack: music for a ceremony; music to talk against; music to dance to.

I phone colour experts to enquire if my green silk evening dress can be dyed scarlet. No. I trawl through my address book: which friends with decent wardrobes are the appropriate size and colouring for me to borrow from?

Axel peers over my shoulder: 'You're becoming obsessive.'

'I want it to be a really special.'

'You'll be free: isn't that special enough?'

'Sometimes people need the positive side of misfortune spelt out for them.'

'Is that what happened with you?'

'No, Axel: but I've never needed help with spelling.'

Maddie bounds in, breathless: 'I feel so guilty that I'm not seeing you these days.'

'You're a budding TV star.'

Collapsing on the sofa, she says: 'They never told me how much work was involved. I had to do four bloody ducks in the end: what a nightmare. I'm completely behind with my column.'

I laugh at the obvious pleasure contained in her complaint and give thanks that the tensions and fears of previous weeks have been cast aside. I say: 'You're thriving on it, Sis.'

'Is that what you think?'

'It's what she knows,' Gavin says, entering the room behind us. 'You know what, Nina – I didn't get to taste a single one of those birds. So much for the perks of associated stardom.' He sits next to her proudly as Maddie picks up an old parking ticket from my coffee table and fans herself theatrically.

'So what's this visit in aid of?' I ask.

'We've been thinking about your divorce party,' Maddie says. 'If your court hearing's on December seventh, the Absolute will come through just after. The obvious party date then, is the nineteenth – Buster's Saturday. But that's only six days before Christmas and that's less than five weeks to organise—'

'Slow down, Sis. I've been making lists—'

Gavin grins: 'Throw them away! We wondered if, instead of doing everything yourself, you'd like to have it in the upstairs function room at my club? Our treat, of course.'

Mala rings me from work: 'I can't make tonight. Royals crisis.'

'You can't get away at all?'

'It's a crisis, Nina. Our Royals man is sunning himself in Wagga-Wagga or somewhere, and my best write-through merchant's still legless in The Old Bell after a lunchtime PA reunion. It's like the bloody *Marie Celeste* in here. I've two freelances, the political editor and a kid on work experience desperately trying to nobble Kensington Palace.'

'What shall I do with the ticket?'

'Ask someone else for goodness' sake. Will. Axel. I don't know.'

I walk across the office to where Axel's putting on his coat. 'Axel, do you want to come to the theatre with me tonight?'

'Can't, Darling: hot date.'

It's six thirty and the performance starts in an hour. Virtually all my friends need at least a day's notice to organise babysitting. The rest of the team has gone. I throw my hands in the air despairingly and head back to my desk.

Axel says: 'Why don't you ask the divine Mr Avedon?'

'We haven't spoken since the Grosvenor House do, ten days ago.'

'He's been busy.'

'Then he won't want to come to the theatre.'

'Not *that* busy. He was sitting in his office twiddling his thumbs five minutes ago.'

*   *   *

We walk up Shaftsbury Avenue arm in arm. It feels good. He says: 'Why on earth did you buy tickets for a play on infidelity?'

'It's had great reviews.'

'It's just so close to home.'

'I quite enjoy the resonances. I've detached myself from my own experience: part of the survival process.' Just in passing, I ask: 'Did you learn anything from it?'

He grimaces: 'I liked the way they stripped away the romance, reducing passion to its component parts.' His stride slows at Cambridge Circus. 'When Lois ran off, I felt as if I'd never love or trust again. It's a cliché, but like most men, I'm not good at articulating emotion: I felt like my heart had been ripped out.'

'I remember.'

'Have I known you that long?' We cut down Charing Cross Road. 'Didn't you feel that way about Buster?'

'No; but we were further down the road. If I chose a cliché, it would be "the bottom fell out of my world".'

'And how do you feel now?'

'I don't know; cheated, I suppose; let down. I didn't have a romantic notion that Buster was incorruptible or anything, but I truly believed he'd resist temptation. In a strange way, I've *stopped* feeling since he went. Feeling about him, I mean.'

'Because you're still in love with him.'

I stop and turn to face him because somehow this is important. 'No, I'm not still in love with him. I haven't been for a long, long time. If anything, I've cut off my feelings because I don't want to *hate* him. That's the stage I'm at now. Buster is my greatest regret; my saddest loss; but that's all. My heart is my own, to give as I wish, Paul. I don't want you – or anyone else, for that matter – to think otherwise.'

*   *   *

Maddie pops in with a long list of fingerfoods and buffet specials for my Divorce Party. She holds up a hand as my eyes widen in disbelief. 'Don't say anything. This series is paying very well: it's no hardship.'

'What about the drink?'

'Free for the first two hours, then a cash bar.' She stops and smiles at me: 'Gavin was minded to ask a couple of young chaps from his office. What do you think?'

'You know what they say, Maddie. The more the merrier.'

We stop outside the Hippodrome. Paul says: 'We could eat somewhere round here or . . . we could get a cab back to my flat in Chelsea and have dinner there.'

'It's ten forty. I've got two children – remember?'

'They'll be asleep now.'

'But not in the morning, Paul. If I come to your place, we both know it's not going to stop at eating.'

He's startled: 'I wasn't making any assumptions, Nina.'

'I can't come. Mum only babysits till twelve on a week night.' He's embarrassed. I say: 'But I'd love to have dinner at yours one weekend, Paul – preferably when Buster's got Lilla and Jack.'

Mala summons me for lunch at The Ivy. Miserably, she pushes a clipping from that morning's *Mail* Diary across the table. I read. 'Good Times Grimes! Within moments of meeting at Notting Hill's celebrated Well Hung art gallery, Breakfast TV sexpert Merry Jangles and celebrated novelist Lawrie Grimes were to be seen whispering secretively. The pair, guests at the opening of a decorative penis exhibiton, were clearly in the early stages of Ugandan discussions as they raced off in a black cab.

'The daffy blonde told fellow art buffs that Mr Grimes's first novel, *Mancunian Hinterland*, was the best thing she'd read since *Bridget Jones's Diary*. Last night, the enigmatic Mr Grimes was unavailable for comment.'

'Oh dear.' No response. 'You're really smitten, aren't you?'

She shrugs: 'It wasn't love; but it had some meaning.'

'They're all idiots aren't they?'

'I wrote the book, remember?'

Paul hovers. Like the last time, he kisses me noncommitally. Then, apropos nothing, he says: 'I want to touch you gently.'

I look at him, surprised; uncertain. I wait for some approach, but he doesn't move. He is controlled; watching.

I say: 'Buster's got the children the weekend of the fifth.'

'I'm in Cornwall. It's my mother's seventieth.'

'Then it'll be after Christmas. Because of my party.'

'I can wait. You're worth it, Nina.'

'Am I?' Inside, I'm singing.

Laura and Alan invite me to dinner with their friend Ellen and her husband, the vicar. The new curate has been invited to make up numbers. We talk a lot about commitment and fidelity. About single parenting and boys growing up without fathers.

We share horror stories.

At one point Ellen says to me: 'You'll be all right with little Jack. He's not one of the dispossessed, living in poverty on a rotten estate in the suburbs. He won't end up in a young offenders' institute for stealing drugs.'

I laugh: 'Because he'll be able to afford them?'

'I didn't mean that!'

'I know you didn't. But even cushioned single parents have trouble coping. There's nobody to relieve the stress. Depression gets compounded by the lack of privacy. Everyone suffers.'

Laura says uncomfortably: 'You've never said that before, Nina. You know I'll take the children whenever you want peace.'

'I know, Laura, but the crucial moments tend to come when you can't off-load them: mornings, bedtime, out visiting.'

Ellen sighs. 'Do you think, Nina, if Buster had been religious, it would have made a difference?'

'I don't know. We shared strong moral codes. I'm not sure God could have helped things along.'

The vicar says humorously: 'God's role wouldn't be quite so active. He'd just provide the perspective. Guidance.'

'I suspect, when you lose *your* way, you can't locate God either.'

'Perhaps, though, it would have helped your kids to centre themselves?'

The curate, who's very young, suddenly says: 'Why do we call them kids? A kid is a young goat. We should call them children. We should confirm their status as human beings. Show respect.'

We all turn. I say: 'Why? Will that stop them misbehaving?'

In the calm of his office, Kevin Preston sits back in his seat with visible pleasure. 'So after all those ghastly last-minute arguments, we're almost agreed.'

'I think so. If he pulls a fast one in court, I'm instructing you to stand our ground.'

'Of course. You know, all in all it's been a remarkably civilised negotiation, Mrs Goodholme.'

'Ms Sutra, if you will . . . *Mr* Preston.'

He throws the dregs of his coffee into the rubber plant pot. 'I do sometimes worry that it's been too amicable.'

'You mean, we've kept your bill low by cutting the arguments?'

He laughs out loud. 'Divorce is a terrible thing, Ms Sutra. In the great scheme of things, yours has effectively been painless.'

The children are asleep. I'm writing my final party-invitation list. Perversely, I pull out my wedding photos to see if anyone's been left out. So many in the group shots are long forgotten. Friends moved on; estranged; people significant for a brief pinprick in time. It all seems so long ago. Even *I* look different.

Granny Sutra is dead now. So too are many of the elderly from both families: Aunty Violet, Uncle Freddie, Mrs Carbody.

I look at Buster: so young. Smiling as we emerge from beneath the crossed gladioli of the BCAF crowd. Cathy there in the middle, understated in beige. Tony Casey at the front – I was so honoured – with Samir, now one of the management team. And Kaz who drowned off the west coast of Ireland. No Paul. He was in the Caymans.

There's a big one of Mala and Jay and Buster and me: arms around each other, faces split wide by our grins. What were we laughing at? Some joke about the kid who comes home and says he's going to be the husband in the school play, and his dad says: 'Couldn't you get a speaking part?' Jay's joke.

There's Liz with Eric – the man she should have married. John, Buster's best man: a smoothie who gives gift-wrapped cars to his women. And Maddie and Gavin, a year before they finally tied the knot; kissing behind a tree. So weird.

I have lost the connection between the celebration on that hopeful and hopeless September day, full of fresh faces and the beloved old; and the event I'm planning now. I strive for a strand that ties the two occasions together, but there isn't one. I realise suddenly that the forthcoming party isn't for what was, or what might have been. It's for what is.

It's entirely for me. A celebration of the new me.

The Decree Absolute isn't relevant to it – because my marriage is meaningless. It's gone. Another life. Another lifetime.

In the bed their father uses during his access weekends, Jack and Lilla are snuggling together. Lilla says: 'Jack just said that when he marries he'll have nine children.'

'Goodness! Who'll look after them, Jack?'

'Daddy.'

'I'm not sure Daddy would like that.'

Lilla says: 'Granny can look after them. Daddy will have children of his own by then.'

She smiles at me, pleased with her reasoning. I'm cold inside. I say: 'Lilla, you and Jack *are* children of Daddy's own.'

'I know Mummy, but I mean ones that'll live with him.' I turn to leave the room. She says: 'I hope he has girls, don't you?'

I can feel tears rising behind my eyes. I say truthfully: 'Now your Daddy's gone, I really don't care what happens to him.'

Maddie's already at the hire shop when I arrive. She says: 'I've shortlisted a vampy scarlet evening dress; two fairy-type outfits for the bridesmaids and a red veil.' Seeing my face, she stops. 'What's wrong?'

'I've decided to abandon the Divorce idea.'

'You're cancelling the party?'

'No. I'm just changing the brief. I don't want to com-memorate an ending: I want to celebrate new beginnings.' I ignore her confusion. 'It's a party, Maddie, not a wake!' A rack of Scarlet O'Hara dresses is wheeled in. I finger a plush blue velvet: 'This would look great on you.'

'It's too dressy.'

'Try it on. Please.' We're like kids with a dressing-up box: except, as kids, I was always the one to pull on the costumes while she directed the productions. Bergman and Bergman. In the blue, she looks sensational. Her new on-screen chignon gives her a neck like Nefertiti; her eyes are sparkling. I watch her shimmy across the room. I say: 'Maddie, is there something you want to tell me?'

'There's nothing I want to tell you.'

She's glowing as if someone's pressed an internal light switch. I'm suddenly confused. She's been working hard. The phonecalls have dwindled. I've barely seen her in weeks. She's like a new person. There's a confidence about her; a frisson of excitement. She's . . . unMaddieish. She catches my eye in the mirror. And stops. I say: 'Maddie, you're having an affair, aren't you?'

Turning down Axel's offer of a drink, I head into Piccadilly. December is here. I've started lunchtime forays to amass Christmas presents: dozens of silly little ones for the children's stockings, and exchangable goodies for friends, family, neighbours and well-wishers.

I'm earning now, but I've also shelled out for clothes, travel and cosmetics. I'm paying Laura for childcare, and evenings out don't come cheap when you're too old for a Wimpy. Plus, Buster's only giving us a slice of his humungous salary when, for years, we effortlessly got through the whole pie.

One day, in Hatchards, I start to panic. It strikes me that I can't actually afford to do things with the same flourish as has been the tradition in our house. I put down the pile of books in my arms and walk out in a daze. I cancel meeting Liz: 'I'll see you at the weekend anyway, so I thought I'd stay in and put my feet up.'

I sit in the study in a cold panic, wondering why I've

never actually gone through the standing orders from the joint account; never actually totted up total spending on food or petrol or bills. Bizarrely, and partly because Buster still has some input, I have no idea how much it costs us to live.

In the middle of a pile of papers I find two unpaid parking fines: £120. I think: I haven't put away any money for tax. I sit in the dark, shaking – not like a leaf but a demented donkey.

Buster says casually: 'I don't understand your urgency for closure. It's not as if I'm not paying maintenance.'

'I need to know exactly how I stand. Anyway, it's too late now.'

'I'm just making a point.'

'Having regrets, Buster?'

'You know I have regrets.'

'That's life, huh?' I store the shopping away in the fridge: tortelloni, nuggets, fishcakes, pies. Instant meals for the children of busy mothers. Upstairs, they're waiting for their father to put them to bed. I say: 'Are you panicked about marrying Christine once the court hearing's over?'

'I've never said anything about marriage.'

'It's the logical step. It squares the circle.'

'Why do you make everything into an argument?'

'What argument? I'm just wondering what's happened to all that animal passion you were enjoying a few months ago. As I recall, you said you'd never felt like that about anyone else.'

'I was crazy then. I told you.'

'So you *are* running scared?'

'What do you know, Nina?'

I turn away: 'Nothing. But I wonder why you deliberately delayed every transaction in the divorce.'

'That's only because your solicitor's so unreasonable.'
'If he's so unreasonable, why have you agreed everything? Pull the other one, Buster, it's got bells on.'

My mother says: 'Yes, Maddie is looking wonderful. I
can't wait for the series to start. It's the talk of the
street.'
'But don't you think there's something *different* about
her?'
'What are you trying to say, Nina?'
'I'm wondering if something's happened.'
'If she's found another man, you mean?' I hold my
breath. She shrugs. 'I think these things are best left to
fizzle out, don't you? If we leave alone, she'll be right as
ninepence by the end of the month.'
'What have *you* noticed?'
She shakes her head: 'Motherly intuition. She's distracted
around Gavin and the boys; lost in thought; different.
Creeping off to make phonecalls. Work, she says, but why
whisper if it's work? Why shut doors?' I struggle to say
something. My mother purses her lips: 'Stay out of it,
Nina. It'll be nothing more than a hankering after some
fancy man. If you make a fuss, she'll take it further. The
important thing is, she won't leave. She's got children. They
always hold the women back.'

Buster says: 'You must know I miss you.'
   I say: 'Of course you miss me, Buster. I was the best thing
that ever happened to you: and you were the best thing that
ever happened to me. It's just so sad that you lost sight of
why we married. And it will be more sad when, one day,
you remember.'
'Do you really think that will happen?'
'Yes I do. And I think that when it does, you will hate
Christine for giving you licence to leave us.'

'I could never hate Christine.'

'Because right now she's all you've got. When you're able to look back without feeling defensive, you'll wonder why she didn't love you enough to let you go. To let you stay with your children.'

'And what would have happened to us?'

'We'd have come through it, stronger and more in love than ever. There was so much there.' He slumps. I say: 'And if we didn't, Buster, it wouldn't have been for lack of trying. We could have held our heads up instead of suffering the pain and the humiliation you brought upon us all.'

I lie in the dark and I cry.

Real tears. Real misery. The first time in months.

I can hear Lilla snuffling in her bed. Jack has crept in with me and is curled asleep against the small of my back.

I cry for my children and what they have lost. Innocence; certainty; confidence; a man.

I cry for the woman I used to be.

I cry for the life we used to have. Safe and secure within a community of like-minded families.

And the new one I'm forging. Independent, silent, slotted in around the edges of other people's lives.

I cry for dreams disfigured. For the crushing of qualities I believed in and espoused. Love, trust; honesty; compassion.

I cry for women everywhere because, no matter what, the buck always stops with us.

Mala says: 'So tomorrow's the big day. What a fool Buster's been. Two more children fatherless.' I sigh and lean back in her office chair: a quick lunchtime visit across town. On the desk are tubs of salad from the local take-away: warm duck with rocket in a balsamic vinegar dressing. 'You're depressed, Nina.'

'It's the thought of arguing in a courtroom with the man I once loved. The rug pulled from under our romantic dream. When we've agreed finances, that's it. The end of the road.'

'Would you have it otherwise?'

I open a tub: 'If I could return to the beginning and start again.'

'Right to the beginning or just the beginning of this year?'

'The beginning of this year.' The salad is delicious; light but filling. I crunch my way through it. 'You know, Mala, I wonder now, if I hadn't reasoned with him; if I'd kneed him in the bollocks, ripped up his suits, stuck his yoga mat down the bog and screamed blue murder, would he have stayed? I appealed to his mind, but by his own admission, he'd lost it.'

She shrugs, standing by the window overlooking Blackfriars Bridge. 'Who can tell? How do you pin a wave upon the sand?' As she turns, her face is full of concern: 'It's going to be hard, Nina. Up to now you've been doing a Schwarzenegger – picking up the ammo and running into the jungle to save what you can. When that piece of paper comes through next week, it's suddenly going to hit you that you're really on your own, Kiddo.'

I nose the car into the courtyard of a small building off Wandsworth High Street. City Life TV studios. Popping a chocolate in my mouth, I park within sight of the entrance. The court hearing is over. I am a free woman. I'm part ecstatic, part terrified. More than anyone else, I want to be with my sister. I leave the engine running and slip in a tape: Oasis, 'Don't Look Back in Anger'.

I call Gavin from my new mobile and tell him I'm diverting her for party talk. Maddie has okayed the menus: trays of chicken tikka, devils on horseback, battered prawns, chicken satay. Later, cold meats and plain salads. Then cheesecake or tiramisu. We've agreed the clothes at a reduced hiring fee. A seventies disco is being organised: Eye to Eye Contact. Instead of these certainties simplifying the process, it suddenly seems ten times more complicated. Half those invited haven't bothered to respond, taking it as read that I know they'll come. Anxiety fodder. At home, Mum is putting the children to bed. I can't face their gentle sweetness, their implicit trust. I wonder where Maddie's got to.

Twenty minutes on, I'm fidgety. It's cold. I don't want to barge in and upset any post-studio conflabs. Part of me wonders if she's somewhere in a side room passionately kissing her producer or director or researcher or cameraman or . . . whatever. I laugh at myself. At us. It's cold in the car. I blow on stiff fingers for warmth.

'Come on, Nina. I haven't got all day.'

'All right.' I pick up the deck and shuffle. I ask: twenty-four hours into my new existence, what does the immediate future hold? The question offers itself in various forms: what will happen in the next twelve months/will everything work out for the best/will I regain my equilibrium? Finally, satisfied, I put the cards down.

'Now divide them into three piles and replace them in any order you want.' I do as I'm told. Cathy picks up the deck and lays out six cards in the pattern of the cross with four supplementaries going up the right-hand side.

There's movement at the door. Bizarrely I turn down the in-car stereo as if it could be heard at that distance. Maddie comes out with a young girl in a puffa jacket and jeans. I feel warm inside at the sight of my sister. She's laughing. She and the girl talk animatedly for a few minutes, then wave goodbye. Maddie walks, unwittingly, in my direction.

Suddenly the girl calls out and comes running back. Maddie looks around. She holds out her arms. The young blonde rushes into them. A warm hug. And then a kiss. With open mouths.

A kiss with open mouths.

From friendly to explosive in seconds.

'King of Cups dead centre: that's you. It's a very male card: to do with emotions. I think, Nina, you've been dealing with your problems in a very male way.' Cathy ponders: 'What I'm saying is, you haven't sat around crying. You've partied: like a bloke.'

'I hadn't quite seen it that way, Cathy.'

'Well, girls usually pick over the pieces don't they? They try and find out what went wrong – but you only look ahead.'

'I get a lot more done that way.'

'Whatever. Anyway, now you're divorced, the tarot's telling you to get in touch with your female side. Soften up.' She moves across the deck: 'The two of cups here, is your marriage. It signifies the couple. It's a good card, but in your case it's a sign of the past; the loss of something precious.' At this I wipe a stray tear from my cheek. She's surprised. 'It matters, then?'

'Of course it bloody matters, Cathy. I married for life, not just for Christmas. But that's gone, hasn't it?'

I toot the horn.

Maddie and the girl look up; startled. Embarrassed.

In the dark she can't see it's me. They both approach the car. I wind down the window: 'I think you'd better get in, Sis.'

'Nina? Dear God! What the hell are you playing at?'

'That's my line isn't it?'

She turns: 'Nadine, this is Nina. I've told you about her.'

'Pleased to meet you, Nina.'

'Well I'm not bloody pleased to meet you.' Silence. Maddie's mouth has gone like a bulldog clip. The girl is hovering. I say: 'Get in, Maddie, or I'll put my hand on the horn and keep pressing.'

'The ten of cups is still about the past – and again it's the loss of love. The wrench in your life. It's all true, isn't it? But up here is the King of Coins followed by the seven of wands: looks like a rich boyfriend, Nina – someone offering security.' A pause; a giggle: 'Paul?'

'Give it a rest, Cathy.'

'And here we have the ten and then eight of coins: you're going to be in the money, Nina. When does Bugle Direct expand?'

'Don't even mention it.'

'This is the Priestess. She's the answer to your question.'

'I've forgotten what the bloody question is.'

We drive in silence for twenty minutes.

Eventually I pull into a darkened square off Camden Road and turn the engine off. 'So what's going on, Mads?'

'You saw for yourself.'

'Well, we've had the *Galloping Gourmet* and *Ready Steady Cook*; next on the menu, Maddie Sutra with Light Lesbian Lunch.'

'Very droll, Nina.'

'What the fuck are you PLAYING at, Maddie?'

She turns coldly away from me, staring out at passers-by. Two minutes, marked by the dashboard clock, pass in silence. I try to stay calm. I say: 'Madeline, you're a married woman with two children. You are just about to launch a new strand in your career. It's not the best moment in your life to discover Sapphic love.'

And then I get the giggles; and I laugh so much, I'm crying.

'The Priestess is the rediscovering of your feminine side.'
    'Fluttering eyelashes – that sort of thing?'
    'It's spiritual, Nina. Maternal. Inner resources. Aura.'
    'It sounds very new age.'
    'Well it is a new age for you, isn't it?' Cathy points to the final card: the scales of justice. 'Ultimately this is a good hand if you've got right on your side, Nina. Act wisely. Once you've sorted yourself and the children out, you won't be unhappy with what fate has in store for you.'

I say: 'Look Maddie, I'm not sitting in judgement. I've learned the hard way that these things happen. But we both know how strong feelings escalate. You've so much to lose.'
    'I didn't go looking for it. It just happened.'
    'Then you'll have to make it *un*happen.'
    'Why? It's not as if I'm planning to run off. I'm not Buster. Nadine and I make each other happy. Nobody's harmed.'
    'Have you slept together?'
    'I haven't spent a night with my arms around her. I haven't woken up next to her. We haven't shared breakfast. But we've . . . pleasured each other, if that's what you're asking.'
    'That must have been a relief after years of celibacy.' She shrugs. 'But that doesn't make it right, Maddie.'
    'What do you know, Nina?'
    'Enough to say that if you don't stop now, you'll bring misery on to yourself, your kids and your husband. A man can live with that sort of guilt, Sis, but I don't think you can.'
    'Why should it only be men who can do it, Nina?'
    'Because that's the way it is.'

*   *   *

Making my way home, I bump into Paul at the lifts. 'How was your mother's birthday, Paul?'

'Dull. Inevitable really, when everyone's reliving the old days.'

'I always enjoy that sort of thing.'

He makes a face. 'I suppose I do, too. It was just that my mother seemed terribly frail all of a sudden. It made me aware of her mortality – and the fact that one day I'd be alone.'

'No brothers or sisters?'

'A brother in Australia. He runs a motorbike service to Ayers Rock.'

'A sort of elderly Hell's Angel?'

'He's only forty-four, Nina. And no kind of angel.' He smiles: 'By the way, how's your sister doing? I was reading about her TV series in one of the papers.'

My mother is asleep on the sofa.

Gently I shake her awake: 'I'm back, Mum. You can get off.'

'What time is it?'

'Only ten o'clock. Maddie was in a rush.' I bend down and kiss her: 'You know I'd go off my head without your help, don't you?'

'You don't have to tell me that, Darling. I remember the lonely years after your father died.' She holds me against her as if I might fly out of her arms like a Sky Dancer: 'I'm so glad the court hearing's over. You're one in a million, my darling.' She gets her coat: 'Do you need me this weekend?'

'I'd quite like to see the girls on Saturday night, if that's all right? You could stay over.'

Again she squeezes me against her: 'I'm your mother. I'd do anything for you, Nina; you know that.'

*   *   *

It's dark and we've detoured into St James's Square itself. The rain has temporarily abated. The bench is wet. Paul is wearing a dark overcoat. I've got on a waterproof Morgan mac that seems to repel water and heat in equal parts.

I say: 'I'm sorry about this, but when you asked about my sister . . . It's too close to home; you know.'

'What's too close to home?'

'Maddie's become a lesbian.'

There's a long silence. Then he says: 'Oh dear.'

'She has a fantastic husband and two brilliant kids and she loves them. But she also loves a twenty-three-year-old food stylist called Nadine.' He says nothing. 'Maddie's like a knotted rope, Paul. She's pulled tight; rigid. This whole thing's out of character. That's what frightens me. She says it's all under control – but what about the girl?'

'How did it start?'

'They had a drink together after filming. That in itself is weird: Maddie hates pubs. And then, she says, it was a goodnight kiss that became something more. Too much more.' In the square a taxi driver shouts abuse at a red Jaguar. I breathe in the smoky, drizzled, November air. 'She doesn't realise what a risk she's taking.'

Paul says: 'Sometimes outcomes are only obvious to people on the outside.'

'You mean that when you're actually shagging away from home, there's a Bermuda Triangle consuming common sense?'

'That's one possibility.' He fidgets: 'I don't know what to say really, Nina. Apart from "sorry".'

'Why are *you* sorry?'

'Because I see nothing but trouble ahead.'

Inexplicably, I have cried more with laughter than sadness in the months since Buster went. The best medicine –

isn't that what the *Reader's Digest* calls it? On that basis, I'd promised myself no jokes in this part: we don't need medicine any more because we're on the road to recovery. But Maddie's taken us slightly off track. And anyway, this one's a cracker.

A woman meets an old friend on the street: 'Sharon! You look terrible! My God, your eyes are blacked, your nose is bent – what the hell's going on?'

'It's Colin. He's started beating me up. I just have to look at him the wrong way and the fists come out.'

Her friend is aghast: 'You have to put yourself first. You're covered in bruises. You must have lost fifteen pounds. Sweetheart – you can't stay!'

Sharon sighs and nods: 'I know; I'm not stupid. I'm just hanging on till I lose another five pounds and then I'm going.'

Paul walks me to the station. 'Were you serious about doing something on your next child free weekend?'

'Were you?'

He looks awkward. 'I don't want to push things, Nina. If you'd like to take this relationship further, let's do that. But if you have reservations, you won't hurt my feelings by stating them.'

'Does that mean that *you* don't have reservations?'

He sighs: 'I'm a man riddled with reservations. On that basis, they're not an accurate depiction of my state of mind.'

I say: 'Speak in English, Paul.'

'I don't have any reservations. No.'

'In that case, why *don't* we do something? Whatever happens, we're old enough and ugly enough to know when something's working and when it isn't.'

As I'm tucking up the children, the doorbell goes: Gavin.

'I've shortlisted two reds and three whites, Nina. I thought you should make the final decision.' I offer him cheese on toast and pour glasses of Chardonnay while he updates me on Dome gossip. 'Just call when you fancy a preview. It's worth seeing.'

Hearing her uncle's voice, Lilla appears at the kitchen door in her nightie. He scoops her into his arms and gives her a kiss: 'You've grown even since I last saw you!'

'Will you put me back to bed, Uncle Gavin?'

'Of course I will, Honeybun. But only one story, okay?'

I wipe down surfaces in a state of anxiety. My brother-in-law is a good, honest, caring man; and he suits my sister perfectly. But they've known each other a long time. They've taken each other's loyalty for granted. Why not? Isn't that the reward for fifteen years together? But now Maddie's got an itch: and the scratching will leave a nasty red weal.

The bread is toasted. I skim slices of cheddar with the potato peeler and cut tomatoes for interest. Upstairs, Gavin is trying to extricate himself. Jack's already fast asleep. Lilla, as always, is anxious to benefit from all and any male input.

He comes back into the kitchen smiling. Dear Gavin. I layer the cheese and tomatoes on the toast and pop the lot back under the grill. 'That looks good,' he says as I dish up.

'Not quite the standard you're used to.'

'We don't get much of that these days.'

We talk wines and make decisions. I tell him about the sale catalogues we're preparing for January mailshots: 'All extremely unglamorous. This is the side of advertising, nobody sees.'

'But it pays the bills?'

'I hope so. I'm only just reacquainting myself with budgeting.'

He smiles. 'We've got more at the moment than we've had in years, but our lives aren't our own any more.'

'Maybe you should go away together? I'd have the boys. Mum would come and help. Why don't you surprise her? A week in Venice or Prague or somewhere?'

'Maddie doesn't get a break until the series is completed.'

'Can't you hustle her off for a couple of days?'

'When? She's filming this Saturday. Next weekend, it's your party.' He sighs. 'She's so busy. She hasn't even made the Christmas pudding yet, and we've already had one drama because I forgot to order goosefat from Lidgate's.'

We laugh. I say: 'You know, Gavin, I really do think you need some time together. I'm very hot on these things since Buster decamped. It doesn't take an awful lot to upset the equilibrium of a marriage – that's why we can never afford to get complacent.'

'Are you trying to tell me something, Nina?'

I shrug: 'Just that emotions are fickle; people are fickle – even Saint Madeline with her passion cake and banana fritters.'

The children and I head off for Laura's: a birthday party. In the sitting room, Marshmallow Fellow is organising a magic show. Laura and I head off into the kitchen. Putting on the kettle, she says: 'I'm exhausted. Alan's parents were down from Monday to Thursday. My cousin and her two kids are coming down on Monday for last-minute shopping. I've been roped in to help with Oliver's class trip to the Rain Forest Café and on top of that, I'm in charge of the church flowers for Christmas Eve.' She pours boiling water into the cafetière. 'It wouldn't be so bad if the car hadn't broken down. I've been piling the kids on the bus for the school run – you try that with a pushchair. There's no such thing as a queue these days.' She slams down the plunger and brings the coffee to the table. Then she loads the dishwasher with various bits of detritus. A child comes in with a request for some string. She pulls a ball from a drawer and sends him on his way. 'I had to get a minicab back from Sainsbury's yesterday – the week's shop plus all the party stuff and three children like wild monkeys around me. Alan did tidy up, bless him, but he's exhausted too. He's getting lots of work that fits around us, but there's been an almighty cock-up on a major accounting programme and they're calling at all hours.' Sighing, she locates cups and pours out. 'The house looks like a breaker's yard. I've got a week's ironing hidden away under the stairs. No school homework's been done and some little vandal's managed to unhook the shower curtain. You weren't happy about returning to work, Nina, but maybe you're having a better time?'

'Mummy, do you remember when you and Daddy were dancing in the sitting room – me and Jack always pushed between your legs so you had to dance with us, too?'
　'Yes, Darling, I do. It was very funny, wasn't it?'
　'And how we'd squash between you in the big bed?'
　'Yes, I do.'
　'Mummy, do you remember last year when you and Daddy took us to Harrods to see Father Christmas? There were two in different rooms, weren't there? And we had those pizzas.'
　'Yes, Lilla, I remember all of that.'
　And so much more.

Saturday night at a seventies disco. Large numbers of men in Shaft wigs and kipper ties wander past. Liz says: 'I don't remember Isaac Hayes in a tie.'
　'This is the *spirit* of the seventies, Liz, not an actual recreation.'

'That explains the dancer in a sixties mini-dress and curly white hairpiece, does it?'

'It's the only thing that can.'

The dance floor is over-subscribed with six foot girls in black halter-neck dresses. 'I feel old,' Mala wails. 'I feel short.'

All the seventies club favourites have been shelved: Edwin Starr; Shalimar; the Real Thing; Barry White. Every second track is Abba. Chart music, not dance music. Play that funky music, white boy. Clutching our drinks we wander aimlessly. Caroline snaps: 'I can live without these trips down memory lane.'

'At least you're not drinking Cinzano and Coke.'

'I never did, Mala. That was your tipple, twenty years ago.'

I say: 'You remember back that far?'

Mala grins: 'I can do better than that. I can remember this actual club. It was called Cinicitta; full of gorgeous young Italians. Sod's law, the only bloke I pulled here was a cheque-book fraudster. Everytime we went to a restaurant, he sat facing the door – in case the police came for him.'

Inexplicably, Liz gets up and jigs around to 'Dancing Queen'. She says: 'I remember one guy I met at the Beat Route. He had a sovereign on his hand as big as my thumb. He drove me home in one of those low red Jags. My Dad came to the door to bawl us out, saw the car and called him in. So weird.'

Caroline says: 'Is that meant to be a joyful reminiscence?'

Mala says: 'These are the only memories that *are* truly joyful. They're about irreverence and irresponsibility. About youth. Later joys come with a price.'

I go out to dinner with Laura. The meal ends at ten thirty.

I say: 'Let's go to Pharmacy and have a drink.'

'I can't do that, Nina. Alan will start to fret.'

'But Laura, this is the first time you've come out in weeks.'

'I'm a married woman. I *want* to get back. It's different for you. You're free to do what you wish.'

But I'm not free to do what I wish.

Liz asks me to go away with her: 'You've been run ragged this year, Nina. Let's go away for a week.'

'Mum's too old to manage the kids that long.'

'Give them to Buster.'

'He won't take them. Besides, how can I have a holiday without Lilla and Jack? They need a break too.'

I am not unattached, because I have two children.

But neither am I *at*tached, because I am free to couple with whoever I choose.

In other words, I am a married woman without a husband: a state of structural limbo which bears the species listing 'Divorcee'.

Caroline is smoking herself on to another plane peopled by women in designer dresses and men with penis extensions parked in their driveways. Mala, Liz and I get up for 'YMCA'. On the dance floor is a pole around which a number of drunken girls are pretend pole dancing with the same gusto that men play air guitars. Legs akimbo, they shimmy up and down in a half daze until, suddenly self-aware, they pull away to giggle with their friends. Tonight's hen-night queen is dressed as a nurse, complete with white stockings and garter. She gives a quick twizzle and is then upstaged by a beautiful young man who removes his T-shirt, undoes his D & G belt and threatens to put us all in a swoon by dropping his trousers. Liz grins: 'Sometimes, don't you wish you could turn the clock back? Be young, be stupid, fall in love over and over again?'

I shake my head: 'Done that. I want to be old, stupid and fall in love over and over again.'

'There speaketh the newly divorced woman.'

I throw back my head and laugh: 'Bloody right. If all ex-wives got pissed and danced, the world would be a brighter place.'

Yes, I believe in life after love.

In the same club where girls gyrate around poles like strippers, others move into each other like small-time porn actresses working themselves up for a lesbian scene. Sometimes it's sexy. Usually it's self-conscious.

Later, at a BCAF function, I meet an old colleague who now works on in-house advertising for a large computer corporation. She'll give me an enormous hug: 'Nina, you look terrific.'

'Not with my clothes off.'

'Will I get a chance to judge for myself?'

I'll laugh: 'You're looking pretty good yourself, Monique.'

After a few drinks she'll come back: 'Now that you're free, you and I should go out together sometime.'

'As long as we're not manhunting, that's fine.'

'Who needs men? Things have changed since you were last single, Nina. These days, anything goes.' She runs a playful finger from my neck to my navel. 'We could have a lot of fun.'

I'll smile uncertainly. 'Has it changed that much?'

'It's what you call mix and match.'

Two hours of nostalgia is sufficient. We pile into Caroline's Alfa TSpark and head for a favourite Soho haunt. It's half past twelve. As we turn into Old Compton Street, Mala's mobile rings. She pulls it open: 'Yes. Chris? What?!' It's fair

to say she's surprised. 'Well, yes, she is. I am. But I can't
. . . not right this minute. I'm in a car full of people. I'll ring
you straight back.'

'What's the matter, Mala?'

'Work.'

Caroline reverses into a space: 'Nina's enquiring about the
nature of the work. You're supposed to have Saturday off.'

'I know, but the second-edition Sundays have just hit the
streets. Lots of exclusives.' She shifts uncomfortably, trying
to climb with dignity from the cramped back seat. 'The night
news editor wants to organise a doorstep for the morning,
but I'm not happy with it.' Stopping under an awning on
the corner of Dean Street, she's back on the phone. 'Can
you get me a decaff?'

As we arrive, a table empties. Liz says: 'It's our lucky
night.'

I'm lying in the steam room when the ghastly Anne-
Marie comes marching in: 'Nina! I didn't see you using
the equipment.'

'Because I didn't.' It's Saturday morning. The children
are in the crèche. I have just one hour to relax.

She slips off her towel exposing a perfect if over-defined
posterior. Carefully she lays it across the wet wooden slats
and lies down, small weights-perfected bosoms pointing
towards the dripping ceiling. 'It's not hot enough.'

'Because you just stood with the door open for five
minutes.'

'I couldn't see who was in here.'

'What does it matter?'

Crossly I find myself holding in my stomach, even though
I'm lying on my back and it's stretched out as much as it
can be. The once thick air has been thinned by the cold
influx from the shower area outside. Anne-Marie does what
appear to be some rapid breathing exercises before turning

on her side, propped on her elbow like a resting guitar, and addressing me through the gloom.

'So how's it going?' I ignore her. 'Abdomen's looking better – still a little buttery when you breathe out.' I close my eyes, thinking about seventies discos and what to wear. She's still talking. I roll on to my stomach in the hope of breaking the flow. There's a minute's silence. Then suddenly she says: 'I hate to mention it, Nina, but have you seen the cellulite on your bum? It's not so much orange peel as the surface of Mars.'

The cappuccinos arrive. Mine is powdered with cinnamon. Mala comes back with a grim look on her face. She sits down and listens to Caroline's monologue on architectural salvage. Liz, currently searching for one-inch Victorian hall tiles, is riveted. Suddenly Mala leans across and whispers: 'Nina I've got to talk to you. Now. Will you come?' We get up. 'Back in a minute.'

We walk towards Wardour Street, moving on and off the pavement as late-night revellers push their way past us. As we pass Rasa Sayang, Mala says: '*The People* are running a story claiming your sister's shagging an MP's daughter.'

'What?!'

'We're going to have to follow it up, Nina. If we'd had it first then maybe . . . I don't know. Maybe I could have conveniently lost it. But now it's out, we've got to chase it like everyone else.'

'She's a bloody food stylist – not an MP's daughter!'

'So it's true?! Shit! Stupid, *stupid* Maddie.' She sighs: 'She hasn't made any comment—'

'She'd deny it anyway—'

'There are photographs, Nina. The two of them embracing at a window. The girl's Nadine Cordwainer. Name ring a bell? Youngest child of the former Foreign Secretary. And, to add to the excitement – she's a reformed heroin addict who once flashed her tits on the Commons balcony.'

'Oh dear God.'

She hands me the mobile: 'Call Maddie and warn her. My boys are already checking it out. By the morning, she'll be under siege.'

Gavin answers the phone. As soon as he hears the screech in my voice he says wearily: 'So you know?'

'Everyone's going to know! Mala says you'll have half of Fleet Street on your doorstep by morning.'

'Are we supposed to pack our bags and flee?'

'Go to your parents, Gavin. Get the kids away from there.' There's a silence at the other end. I say: 'She's completely mad. I don't know what got into her.' No response. 'Gavin, this is nothing. Maddie's menopausal.'

'At thirty-five?'

'I don't know. But you *will* get past this. Honestly.'

'After my whole family's been splashed across every bloody front page in England? What about the boys?!'

'This isn't the time.'

'Did you know, Nina?' I look across helplessly at Mala. 'You did know, didn't you?'

'We can talk later, Gavin. The priority is to get away. I've got your spare keys if you forget anything.'

'What are we going to do?'

'Whatever needs doing, it'll be done.'

The next morning it's in all the late editions. Small snaps of Maddie, blow-ups of Nadine: on the hustings with daddy at twelve; a Youth Theatre production of *Hamlet* at sixteen; derelict in a doorway, high on heroin, aged nineteen; flashing her small and perfectly formed bosoms at twenty; photos show her outraged mother; little side bars regurgitate the conciliatory comments made by her politician father; sad shots of her entering rehab clinics dominate the years between twenty and twenty-two; and then, cleaned up at twenty-three, a relationship with an actor from *The Bill* is mentioned in one of the scandal sheets.

Then nothing.

Three years of food styling for magazines and TV, followed by a crazed lust for Maddie. What a totally bizarre chain of events. A food chain of events.

Coming out of the loo, I find Lilla with *The People*. 'Mummy, what does lesbian mean? Why is Auntie Maddie kissing the lady like that? Is she in a nightie?'

I snatch the paper away. 'You shouldn't be reading that.'

She shrugs. 'Her girlfriend isn't very pretty, is she?'

I close my eyes. Calm calm calm. 'Go and find Jack.'

'I don't want to. Does Uncle Gavin know Auntie Maddie's got a girlfriend? Is a lesbian the same as being gay?'

'I don't want to discuss this with you.'

'I'm gay, you know, Mummy.'

'What?!'

'Well, I love Heba because she's my best friend. So that means I'm gay. I'm going to tell everyone tomorrow.'

'Don't be ridiculous, Lilla.'

'Is it bad?'

I try to gather my thoughts. 'No, Lilla, it isn't, but loving Heba doesn't mean you're gay. That's a *different* kind of love.'

'So does Auntie Maddie love her girlfriend like I love Heba, or is it the different kind of love?'

I shake my head. 'Auntie Maddie loves Uncle Gavin and Charlie and Joe. She's also very fond of her friend, Nadine, but she gave her the wrong kind of kiss and cuddle and because of that, people think she's gay. But she isn't. She's just the same as always.'

Lilla nods, as if she understands, and wanders off.

Maddie rings around lunchtime. Crying. She says: 'I'm sitting in the tack room so nobody can hear me. I can't let Nadine take the flak, Nina. It wouldn't be fair.'

I snort. 'It would be even more unfair if your husband, sons and family had their lives destroyed for her, Sis.'

'You're being inflammatory and unfeeling.'

'No. I'm being blunt. This isn't about you any longer, Maddie. It's about decency and trust and the people who have loved and supported you through your life. If you put Nadine's needs – or even your own – above theirs, all that time and effort has been worth nothing. Effectively, *you* have been worth nothing.'

'You're confusing me with Buster.'

'No. I'm not. Buster lost sight of decency and dignity. You haven't, Maddie. You're still with Gavin and the boys.' She starts to sob down the phone. I cannot remember the last time my sister cried. Perhaps after our father's death; our mother always says Maddie saw it as abandonment and I turned it into a liberation. I say: 'Listen Maddie, you can get over a love affair, but your children won't. If *they* can't touch your heart – is it a heart worth following?'

There's a silence. She says: 'What gives you the right to take the moral high ground, Nina?'

I pause; nonplussed. I suddenly want to reach down the line and rock her in my arms like Lilla or Jack when they're hurting. I say: 'I dont know, Mads. I guess sometimes, when you're pushed into the wilderness, the high ground is the only place that promises safety.'

'I can't see my way there.'

'No.' I sigh; unable to offer anything that could negate the horror; the mess. 'Let's look for it together, Maddie. If we only get halfway there, at least we'll have tried.'

*   *   *

Lilla, Jack and I snuggle up to watch *Matilda*. They love Miss Honey but I prefer the spunky Trunchball who swings children by their plaits and sticks them in the chokey.

I think about seduction and love; about Buster and Maddie: one a very literal man not given to flights of fancy; the other a tightly controlled woman living her life by numbers. Both ill equipped to deal with seduction; both lacking sufficient humility to see the ramifications of their actions.

I pull my children to me, grateful, finally, to be blessed with their presence; long past the resentment of those first months. I smell the Derbac M on their hair and feel fulfilled.

As Matilda's parents disappear into the sunset of neglect, Jack says: 'Mummy, stay with me for ever.'

'Of course I'll stay with you for ever.'

'Why?'

'Why?' I look down at him, confused.

Lilla rolls her eyes: 'Because it's her job, Stupid,' and she gives me the most enormous hug.

Do we need another joke at this stage? Well maybe. As my stupid sister has dragged us back to square one because the sight of a food stylist in winceyette sets her juices flowing.

Isn't it sod's law that just as the rest of us are getting on with our lives, some cantankerous cow goes and spoils it all? I wonder now if Maddie's sexual reticence was down to her being a closet lesbian. No: that suggests a degree of self-knowledge. A coffin lesbian. Dead until someone else prised the lid off.

Bollocks to Buster; molluscs to Maddie. Well, she is a cook.

At this moment, I feel more love for her than in years: perhaps because she's needier than she's ever been. But I'm also angry. Furious. I'd like to pick up one of her latticed semolina crust lamb casseroles and smash it against the pink plaster-finished wall of her Smallbone Shaker-style kitchen.

Monday. Axel watches me drag myself in. 'Another late night?'
　'Late night, early morning. Jack was up at six.'
　'That's the trouble with being single.'
　'No, Axel. That's the trouble with *not* being single.'
　'I saw the papers. Deep dudu ahead.'
　'Can we give the subject a miss for a few hours?'

Oh yes, I nearly forgot the joke. This is it.
　Two women accost a man at the bar in the Hilton. One says: 'Hello, do you come here often?'
　His answer is friendly: 'Actually it's my first time.'
　'Oh. Where do you usually go?'
　He smiles: 'To be honest, I haven't been out in fifteen years.'
　'Why's that?'
　Embarrassed, he says: 'I've been in prison.'
　Unabashed, the woman asks: 'What did you do?'
　He looks away. 'This isn't as bad as it's going to sound, but I killed my wife.'
　Wildly the woman clutches his arm: 'You mean you're single?'
　Onwards and upwards.

I call Gavin at work. He's calm; measured; forcibly in control.
　His wife has issued a denial to the press, claiming Nadine was helping her resolve a life crisis.
　Nadine's father, Hector Cordwainer, is doing a great job, treating it all as a silly joke: naughty daughter in trouble again. She, meanwhile, has taken the first flight out to Mauritius: 'Nadine's been working very hard. She

needed to recharge her batteries. She's been through so much already: this only adds to her stress. Thank you in advance for allowing her space and privacy.'

A TV company spokesman, clearly relishing the exposure, announces that transmission of Maddie's series will begin two weeks earlier than planned. 'This is not a cynical exercise; the decision had already been made on scheduling grounds. It takes more than publicity to hold an audience; Miss Sutra's welcoming kitchen style will mesmerise a new generation of foodies.'

Yeah. Foodies in combat trousers.

Gavin says: 'Five days to the party, Nina. We're covered on all fronts. Don't panic.'

'Don't panic? You shouldn't even be *thinking* about it!'

'It's the only thing keeping me sane. At least there's something to celebrate.'

Yes, Nina Sutra, the gay divorcee.

Whoops. Wrong sister.

Paul finds me at the coffee machine: 'Would you like lunch?'

'I'm going Christmas shopping with Cathy.'

'That's very organised.'

'Her idea. It's kind of you to ask.'

'Who said I was asking out of kindness?'

Tuesday lunchtime, Axel says: 'Kevin Preston's on the line.'

I return to my desk and pick up the phone. Kevin says: 'Your Decree Absolute has been certificated, Nina.'

The final 'i' is dotted. In January this year, I was a happily married woman; a team player. Eleven months later, I am a divorcee. I do not love Buster any more, but if he hadn't gone, I would most certainly have continued to love him as I always did. It says much for what we shared, that despite his departure, I cannot hate him. I replace the receiver.

'Is it through?' I nod. Axel says: 'An ending and a beginning in one day. Come on: it's great news about the Bugle Direct expansion.' I smile, lost in thought. He sings softly: 'It's a little souvenir of a terrible year, that makes my eyes so sore'.

Tin Tin Out: Here's Where the Story Ends.

But it isn't the story that's ended. Just the chapter.

Wednesday. I sit at my desk, thinking. I am a mother. A good mother. A good mother who's too busy just yet to say the magic words – I love you – to someone outside our home. Yet I yearn to be held in the arms of a man who can love not just me, but my children too. A husband; a father.

A man who'll share my chocolate and say: 'Come here and give me a cuddle', or 'Here's a fiver, buy yourself a new dress.'

A man to love and nurture, knowing that the energy and joy he gets from us, is enough to keep him close.

A man who won't go sulking and skulking to a Christine Brown.

Thursday. Maddie calls. 'Susannah picked up the dresses this morning. They look wonderful. I've bought Gavin a new tie.' A pause. 'I think I'm being spied on, Nina. Two men have been sitting outside in a Ford Galaxy all day. They must be journalists.'

'Funny what love can do, Sis.'

'Will you *please* stop the sarcasm! For God's sake, there's enough unpleasantness flying around without your adding to it.'

'Does the fact you've bought him a tie, mean it's all on again?'

'I don't know. How can I know when I'm being hounded both outside and inside my home? I've drawn the curtains.'

'Have you heard from the young tit flasher?'

'What?' An exasperated sigh: 'No. I haven't. The only issue right now is the rest of you treating me like a pariah.'

'Maddie, *we are a family*. Is some mad tart who polishes radishes for a living more important?' I stop. 'Sorry. I'm doing it again, aren't I? It's just – I've already lost Buster. You're my rock. I don't want to lose you.'

She sighs: 'How can you? As you said, *we are a family*.'

Friday. Buster arrives at seven for the handover. Lilla and Jack are watching Disney in the front room. They shout hellos, but don't move. We stand in the hallway looking at each other.

He says: 'So it really is over.'

'Yes.'

He puts his arms out to me and, for the first time since he went, I walk into, and am wrapped in, them. So warm. So strong. So comforting. Somewhere under the buttons of his shirt is that thicket of blond chest hair. Beneath the waistband of the trousers is that little pouch of middle-aged spread. I know his smell so intimately; my head fitting into the well of his shoulder. He buries his nose in my hair and pulls me tighter.

I close my eyes and for one wondrous moment, it's like the past eleven months never happened. Buster has come home from work and is hugging me before going in to roll around with the children and take off his suit and wander into the kitchen to talk about his day. In a minute he will moan about his clerk or tell me some funny snippet of gossip that's come his way. And I, emerging from an afternoon of playing and listening to Lilla and Jack, will regale him with stories about friends, foes, family. Then we'll eat dinner together and curl up on the sofa with books or the TV on, and we'll carry on talking. Like we always did. Every day for ten years.

But that moment; that wondrous moment; is over. And I suddenly realise that, actually, he feels different. His body is harder; his smell is more synthetic; the familiarity is in what he represents, not in what he is. I pull away feeling strange; knowing that I too must feel different. Must *be* different. We smile awkwardly at each other. He says: 'I love you, Nina.' I'm so taken aback, I don't know what to say. I shake my head and turn away. He says: 'I was an idiot. A complete idiot. But we can't turn the clock back now.' A pause. 'You could never find it in yourself to forgive me.'

I stand at the kitchen door. I say: 'In order to be forgiven, you have to first say sorry, Buster. You've never done that.'

'It goes without saying.'

'No; it doesn't.' I turn around and look at him; this man who I lived and breathed and loved for so long. This man who woke up one morning and, without a word of tenderness or regret, walked out on me and our children for a woman he barely knew. I say: 'You're feeling sorry for *yourself*, Buster. Not for me. Not for Lilla; not for Jack. You've never felt sorry for us.' I smile at him. I say: 'Even if I could forgive you, Buster, how could you ever forgive yourself?' Now he shakes his head. Disbelievingly. As if I have thrown something precious back in his face.

'You've just proved my point, Nina.'

'Maddie, you were the one who said we should leave your problems till after the party, okay?'

She sniffs, crossly. 'Fine.'

I sit at the old familiar table and watch as she puts

away the shopping: preserved lemons, Blue Mountain coffee, organic pork, raspberry vinegar, pickled walnuts, baby carrots, grapeseed oil, butternut squash, amaretti biscuits. Upstairs, the boys are already in bed. Gavin is on his way home.

Cosy domesticity.

I meet Mala at the bar in Axis. The room is vast; posturing. She's wearing a dramatically cut Droopy & Brown coat. 'Sorry to drag you out. I was desperate for a drink.'

'That's all right. So was I.'

'Maddie getting on your nerves?'

'Yes. And Buster. He said he loved me.'

She rolls her eyes. 'Withdrawal pangs.'

'Don't worry, I wasn't taken in.'

We order vodkas and loll around, examining the minutiae of our own fractured relationships and those of the people around us. Looking at how an unexpected or insignificant encounter can ultimately provide the gunpowder that detonates even the soundest of unions.

Two men in their early forties approach us and offer dinner downstairs. We smile politely and decline. After they've gone, Mala says: 'I feel too grotty to flirt tonight.'

'I know. Anyway, we need to save our best lines for tomorrow.'

'You've laid on some good talent, have you?'

'You bet I have, Darling: starting with you and me.'

In the background they're playing Des'ree: life, oh life, oh life, oh life, du du du du.

Saturday: Maddie shakes me awake. 'We're late. Come on.' She calls a cab and we rush to the beauty parlour off Ladbroke Grove to spend the next four hours in a state of suspended bliss: steamed, scrubbed and massaged. Our hair is hennaed, our faces pressed and our nails painted.

At the end of the session we're made up by a woman who claims we could both pass for twenty-two. The Sutra sisters are on form!

When we get back, we admire each other in the mirror. Maddie says: 'God, you're beautiful, Nina.'

'So are you. Like a venus from a painting.'

We stare at each other with pride and wonder. And cry. Thank heavens for waterproof mascara.

Lilla calls. 'Mummy, I wanted to tell you that Daddy's bought me a new china doll and Jack's got a batmobile that opens.'

'Aren't you spoilt! What else have you been doing?'

'We met Christine and went to a chocolate factory.'

'I hope you bought some chocolate home for me?'

A pause. 'We forgot.' She's embarrassed.

I say: 'That's all right, silly. I was only having fun.'

'And Daddy says we can go to his flat on Christmas Eve and open our presents there.'

'Does he?' My stomach clutches. Like being caught in a vice.

'Is that all right?'

'I think Daddy should talk to *me* about that.'

'I asked him to come on Christmas Day, Mummy, but he can't because they're going to Manchester.'

I say: 'In that case, darling, of course you must see him on Christmas Eve, but it's too early to make definite plans.'

'Aawww!'

'I'll talk to him about it in the week.' Across the room Maddie raises a quizzical eyebrow. I take a deep breath: 'So what are you doing right now?'

'Daddy's making pasta. He says we can stay up till nine.'

'Lucky you! Is Jack there? I must say goodnight to him.'

'All right. See you tomorrow, Mummy. I love you.'

'And I love you, darling. More than you'll ever know.'

*   *   *

When we get to the club, there are already around thirty people in the big upstairs room, one half of which has a bar and dance floor. They cheer as we go in: here's to you, Nina!

Axel sidles up: 'You're truly ravishing.'

'It's such a shame then, that you're truly gay.'

More people are spilling in: friends I haven't seen for months, all coming up with smiles on their faces, reminiscing, gossiping, regaling me with funny stories. Some bring little presents as if it's a birthday: handmade chocolates; picture frames; a scented penis candle; a frosted vase; *The Little Book of Calm*. Laura has inscribed it. Maybe this will make you a calmer Sutra! And even though I've had the same joke all my bloody life, I laugh.

I'm on such a high, I'm laughing half the night. Even when my mother, resplendent in a frock from Fenwick's, announces loudly: 'Nina's always been a fighter,' I cringe with a smile on my face.

The DJ is getting into his stride. 'I Will Survive' has been banned but he can't resist a few apposite oldies: Johnny Nash, 'I Can See Clearly Now'; Roxy Music, 'Dance Away the Heartache'; Tammy Wynette, 'D.I.V.O.R.C.E'. At this last one I tap him on the shoulder, pull one of the headphones off his ear and shout: 'Give it a rest, will you: we're not all fucking morons!'

He says 'What shall I put on then?'

I think for a moment. 'The Verve. "Bitter Sweet Symphony".'

On the dancefloor, Will's showing off a new girlfriend. He says: 'Don't be such a spoilsport, Nina.'

'Spoilsport? I'm an independent woman, not a walking cliché!'

Gavin's pal David is here with a group of promising bachelors from the Dome. He calls me over and makes introductions. One of them says: 'May I have a dance, later?'

I grin fit to burst: 'That would be lovely.'

Liz is sporting a brilliant new haircut. I pull her into the group and politely exit with a wink to the willing man. I wander round in a little dream like a chipmunk with an over-full stomach. Cathy is proudly clinging on to Richard's arm, talking to the Caseys, her new and miniscule bump straining against the Lycra of her minidress. She's like a pop star. Maturing Spice. Laura and Alan are laughing with Samir and Roni. Janice and Caroline are standing watchfully in the wings. I spot some BCAF talent heading their way. In a corner Mala has been buttonholed by Axel: 'Greetings, Gorgeous.'

I say: 'You look like a pair of conspirators.'

'You mean we look guilty?'

'I've been telling Mala about you and Paul.'

'What about me and Paul?'

Mala says: 'Precisely. *What* about you and Paul?'

I squeeze my best friend's arm: 'Now listen, I've just promised a dance to a hunky architect. Don't go marrying me off.'

'Who said anything about marriage?'

And then I see him at the door; a little frazzled, wet from the winter rain. He waves and heads for me: 'Nina: sorry I'm late. You look . . .' He shakes his head: 'I can't think of anything original. Let me have a drink, then I'll tell you.' I smile and turn away – and am yanked gently back to his side. 'No. I'll tell you now – exquisite. Just lovely.' I stand there awkwardly. Mala and Axel are watching with interest. Paul says: 'Let's not play games. You're free now. I want to spend proper time with you.'

I giggle: embarrassed; thrilled. I squawk: 'Not long to the new year!'

'Do I have to wait?'

I look around at this room full of familiar faces. The faces of people who, when my world threatened to fall apart, came marching out of skirting boards like an army of ants, holding me above their heads until I could stand on my own.

I look across at my mother; my sister; Gavin; all themselves suffering the riptide of our disaster. At my beloved in-laws who've come to celebrate with me. At the many partners I don't know well, who stoically stayed silent when I rang their spouses at midnight because I needed someone to cry with.

There are no tears now. Well, there *are*, but only tears of happiness. We've come through it all together; and we're celebrating. Together.

I throw my arms out because I want to embrace the world.

I say: 'The new year isn't far away, Paul. Why hurry?' And I laugh. 'I've got the rest of my life in front of me.'

∫

Epilogue

On the Monday after the party, I received this e-mail story from a friend in Australia.

DANCE LIKE NOBODY'S WATCHING
Jeff was the kind of guy you love to hate: always in a good mood and always positive. When someone asked him how he was doing, he would reply, 'If I were any better, I'd be twins!'

He was a unique restaurant manager because his waiters followed him around from job to job. They liked his attitude. He was a natural motivator, always finding good in bad.

Seeing this style really made me curious, so one day I went up to Jeff and asked him: 'I don't get it! How can you possibly be so positive all of the time?'

Jeff replied: 'Each morning I wake up and say to myself, "Jeff, you have two choices today. You can choose to be in a good mood or you can choose to be in a bad mood." I choose to be in a good mood. Each time something bad happens, I can choose to be a victim or

I can choose to learn from it. I choose to learn from it. Every time someone comes to me complaining, I can choose to accept their complaining or I can point out the positive side of life. I choose the positive side of life.'

'It's not always that easy,' I protested.

'Yes, it is,' Jeff said. 'Life is all about choices. When you cut away the junk, every situation is a choice. You choose how you react. You choose how people will affect your mood. You choose to be in a good mood or bad mood. The bottom line is: *It's your choice how you deal with life.*'

I reflected on what Jeff said.

Soon after, I left the industry to start my own business. We lost touch. Then, several years later, I heard that Jeff had done something you never do in the restaurant trade: he'd left the back door open one day and been held up by three armed robbers. While trying to open the safe, his hand was shaking so much, he missed the combination.

The robbers panicked and shot him.

Luckily, Jeff was found relatively quickly and rushed to the local trauma centre. After eighteen hours of surgery and weeks of intensive care, he came out with bullet fragments still in his body.

I saw Jeff about six months after the accident. When I asked him how he was, he said, 'If I were any better, I'd be twins!'

I shook my head and asked what had gone through his mind as the robbery took place. He said: 'The first thing that went through my mind was that I should have locked the back door. Then, as I lay on the floor, I remembered that I had two choices: I could choose to live, or I could choose to die. I chose to live.'

'Weren't you scared? Did you lose consciousness?' I asked.

Jeff laughed: 'The paramedics were great. They kept telling me I'd be fine. But in the emergency room I saw the expressions of the doctors and nurses and got really frightened. In their eyes, I read, "He's a dead man." I knew I had to take action.'

'What did you do?' I said.

'Well, there was a nurse shouting questions at me. When she asked if I was allergic to anything, I replied: "Yes." They all stopped. I took a deep breath and yelled, "Bullets!" Over their laughter, I told them, "I am choosing to live. Operate on me as if I am alive, not dead."'

Jeff lived, thanks to the skill of his doctors, but also because of his amazing attitude.

I learned from him that every day we have the choice to live fully. Attitude, after all, is everything.

You now have two choices:

1. Save or delete this mail from your mail box, or
2. Forward it to people you care about.

I hope you will choose number two.

I'm forwarding this to you.

> Work like you don't need the money
> Love like you've never been hurt
> Dance like nobody's watching

$\int$

Acknowledgements

Thank Yous from the bottom of my heart to Martina and Miriam, who've given so much time to turn me round. To my Mum, Mallika, who is, and does, everything. Susan for tea and sympathy. Nicola for weekend bedspace. Frazer who supplied many jokes and e-mail homilies. And all friends and family, mainly female, who've been there for me and the children.

Hail the sisterhood. Let's party!